Finding Words in Whitechapel
and other stories

Sydnee

Sydnee Blake

Finding Words in Whitechapel

Sydnee Blake

Copyright © 2013 Sydnee Blake

The moral right of the author has been asserted.

Apart from any fair dealing for the purposes of research or private study,
or criticism or review, as permitted under the Copyright, Designs and Patents
Act 1988, this publication may only be reproduced, stored or transmitted, in
any form or by any means, with the prior permission in writing of the
publishers, or in the case of reprographic reproduction in accordance with
the terms of licences issued by the Copyright Licensing Agency. Enquiries
concerning reproduction outside those terms should be sent to the publishers.

Matador
9 Priory Business Park
Kibworth Beauchamp
Leicestershire LE8 0RX, UK
Tel: (+44) 116 279 2299
Fax: (+44) 116 279 2277
Email: books@troubador.co.uk
Web: www.troubador.co.uk/matador

ISBN 978 1783063 505

British Library Cataloguing in Publication Data.
A catalogue record for this book is available from the British Library.

Typeset in Times New Roman by Troubador Publishing Ltd

Matador is an imprint of Troubador Publishing Ltd

For Joy, Aden, Felix and Rachel

Contents

Finding Words in Whitechapel	1
Highbury Fields, *a sentimental tale*	13
A Jazzy Evening in Old New York	27
The Roofer	32
Lacrimae	39
Hungarian Teeth	56
Lou-Lou's History of Money	66
A Part to Play	72
Aim High	78
Tom Downey-eiderdown	91
The Death Hat	107
The Yellow Brick House	123
The Home Boys	134
To be a Pilgrim	141
The Ladies Play Poker	149
Always Peaceful in Mont Plaisir	161
A Prize	171
Dressed in vanilla-white	175
The Case is Altered	180
The Geography Lesson	186

Finding Words in Whitechapel

July 1903

Sweat-dripping heat. Lining up, Isaac peered from behind J. Rosen's wide back and silently urged Mr Usherwood to ring the school bell. Nothing happened, although the sun was burning a hole in his thick school cap and into his melting brain. Of course caps must always be worn because Jewish boys covered their heads to respect God, but why can't He help him today and make time move? Didn't He know something strange was happening at home? Shifting from leg to leg, Isaac reversed the word BOYS, which was scrolled in wrought-iron letters over the school gate and let SYOB hiss and slither through his lips. But the Headmaster didn't stir.

Something important was happening about his brother. He couldn't wait here doing nothing. Making his body supple like a Mohican Indian, Isaac traced Mr Usherwood's every movement. He mimicked the arm in the black sleeve suspended in the air. At last it fell and rose, the metal clapper hitting the bell again and again, sounding 'school dismissed' over the playground. T. Arnold led the surge to the gate, followed by the other thudding feet of 6 Standard. Finally he, I. Rosenberg filed by, but once outside the gate flew swift as an arrow.

Ignoring the boys who were pushing into the nearby streets, he flashed past Schlomo's Shoe Repair, and Gertie's

Dress Shop, then sped down Woodseer Street. Sweat was dripping off his nose as he raced down Brick Lane, his brain whirring – why was his little brother being moved from their room? The familiar Whitechapel tram bells were ringing as he darted between the different barrows filled with vegetables, dress goods, pots and pans. Now breathless, he stopped for a moment to inhale the yeasty smell rising from kegs left on the wooden carts. Around him voices sang 'Alte zacha', 'Shmaltz herring', 'Pretzels, two for ha'penny'. His mouth watered, but his pockets were empty, so he looked around to find a way to cross the busy Whitechapel Road.

Worrying questions flashed again – his brother was being moved, mama and papa were always quarrelling. Why? But no, he must concentrate now. Watch! There was a tram moving along the track towards him, if he ran quickly he could cross. Not difficult because the horse in front of him was standing still as stone. Ready, steady – but just then its tail went up and out dropped steaming muck, before the horse moved on. Still, he must cross! And clutching his books Isaac leapt over the shiny brown balls, dashed behind a hackney cab that was trotting the other way, and with lungs whistling for breath reached the other side of the road. The tram bell clanged angrily at him. But he must take chances; it's what people had to do. Victorious, he dangled his schoolbooks over his shoulder, and sped on towards home.

Again the worry – David wasn't ill, yet this morning before school his straw pallet was taken out of the room they shared and brought into Mama's and Papa's. No reason had been given him, and that wasn't right.

Isaac ducked between the women busy moving around Mr Hakeem's barrow with its beautifully ordered fruits – pyramids of shiny lemons, sunny oranges, clutches of purple grapes. Eyes half-closed he drank in the sweet tempting smells, and barely avoided falling over a pile of chicken heads left to rot in the sun!

With a last spurt he reached the blue sign of Miller's Milk Store, and turned down into the familiar noise of Jubilee Street. Here he joined children from other schools and ran on until he reached the crumbling name of Jubilee Mansions. The door to the small ground floor flat was always open and waiting in the kitchen would be Mama and his sister, both sitting at the table sewing for Mrs Cohen and Mrs Loewy.

'Mama,' he called, and ran over with a quick kiss. Then he saw his father was in his corner reading his beloved Tolstoy. 'Papa – I didn't expect you to be here,' and felt the hard bristles of his father's beard against his cheek.

Without looking up, his father said, 'Too hot today to go out peddling buttons and ribbons.'

'Isaac, take off your jacket and cap. It's hot.' With relief, he hung them on the nail behind the door. 'Have water. Minnie, fill a pitcher, get a glass for your brother.'

'Mama, I'll go …'

But Minnie had put down the blue silk blouse she was working on and was already at the kitchen tap. Waiting, she took off her glasses and wiped them, squinting in the afternoon light.

Mama stopped sewing and examined him. 'How was school today?'

'Good. In English we did grammar, parsed sentences. Then Mr Usherwood read a poem by a poet called John Keats. Minnie, I have a bad memory, can only remember a few lines, but listen – *To Autumn – Season of mists and mellow fruitfulness Close bosom-friend of the maturing sun.* Then the words were gone. What were they? Again he went over the lines in his mind...*Conspiring with him to load and bless with fruit the vines that round the thatch-eaves run.*' He searched, but the rest had slipped away. 'How stupid, I can't remember any more. *Mellow* is ... soft, like your voice, Minnie ... See, we are sharing pictures and thoughts with John Keats. Isn't that wonderful? Words like *bosom-friend*, the autumn produce is tied to the helpful sun and how *to load* and *bless* our ordinary lives. Your eyes and nose know because he speaks of the roots of things. Can you imagine, people see all that in the countryside? I'll borrow the poem from the library, learn it, then we can understand all the special meanings and sounds of his words.' He couldn't stop himself and told them how Mr Usherwood let him draw in his study at break, that he commended his sketch of Baby Annie.

'You're a good boy. I'm proud of you,' his mother nodded to him, then picked up the skirt and continued sewing her tiny stitches. 'Today Minnie put kerosene on your mattress, then aired it. A lot of bugs dead. You'll sleep better.'

That was good news and having been reminded of last night, he reached behind to scratch his back. Minnie returned with the pitcher and handed him a full glass. He lightly touched her callused fingers. 'Thank you, dear Minnie-Pinnie,' and sat down at the table and drank until he was full. Talking and the water made him feel better, but looking at his mother he knew something was not right, even though Minnie was smiling at him as she took up her needle.

It was hard to keep sitting, waiting for his mother to say why David had been moved. She'd nearly finished doing the hem, and after the last in and out, the final loop, she cut the thread, put the needle in the box.

'Mrs. Loewy has an important meeting tomorrow night, so I'll put the lace collar on the blouse after supper,' and she gently folded the blue silk into a piece of tissue paper. 'Isaac, before I go over to Mrs. Schiff's for Annie and David, I must have a word. You won't like it, my dear son, but it has to be.'

She pushed herself up, went over to the black stove, picked up a wooden spoon and started to stir the soup. The delay stirred him, too, made him want to shout 'hurry', but instead he kept on watching.

'We are having a lodger. Mr Abou Saleem is coming. He's arrived from the Kashmir, and is to sleep in your room with you. His cousin sells fruit. He has eight children and his wife in one room. They have no place for him, so each night Mr Saleem sleeps here, he pays. There is more money.'

Trapped.

From the corner, his father's deep voice said, 'I am sorry, Isaac.'

His mother turned to him, her face twisted like a pretzel, 'You are sorry? You are sorry? It's your fault! What kind of man are you, never going out selling, never bringing in money? Instead always reading. Selfish. Selfish. Never thinking of your family. You know what I call you – a shtick drek!'

Without lifting his eyes, his father answered quietly, 'You are a bad Jewish wife, who does not honour her husband.'

Always the same – no money – no love.

'Isaac, Mr Saleem will be here after supper. Now, I'm going to fetch the children. Minnie, fix the soup for your brother, we have eaten. There's also a piece of bread for you.'

'Mama, perhaps Isaac would like to go to his room first, do some homework, then eat?'

'Yes, yes,' and she left.

Isaac picked up his books and closed the door behind him. At thirteen he must not cry. But there was a cutting pain in his throat. He looked around at the walls, the chipped plaster – his and David's room. No, no that wasn't it, and he went over to the orange crate near the open window. This was what mattered – his best drawings, all gathered together in a grey folder that Mr Usherwood had given him. Now to be shared with a stranger. These were his precious books all ordered neatly in a short row, mostly prizes from school. He reached for the book borrowed from Whitechapel Library, the one he was reading, and leafed over the pages of *The Call of the Wild*. Thornton, the master, Buck, the dog. He quickly closed it. No, he must do his arithmetic, go over history: Pitt the elder, Pitt the younger, get them firmly in place, then as a reward read about Buck.

He sat down on his pallet near the window, looked over at the empty space where David usually slept, where they hunted as Indian trappers, men searching for the gleaming gold in the icy north of Alaska. Forget that now, he told himself, and untied the rough rope around the books and his slate. Numbers first, and he fished in his pocket to find a short piece of chalk.

A light knock on the door, and Minnie came into his room. 'Are you almost finished? Mama's putting Annie and David to bed. It's time for your soup.'

Isaac nodded, then in a whisper, 'Minnie, I just want to know, why are we so ...' but looking into her thick lens, her distant eyes, he couldn't finish the sentence. He followed her to the table, sat down and quickly ate his beet soup and bread. He was scraping the sides, when there was a knock. His mother closed the bedroom door firmly behind her and opened the front door.

'Mrs Roseberg?'

'Rosenberg. Come in, Mr Saleem. We have just finished supper.'

The man stood by the door and tried to make a little bow, but over his shoulders was strapped a small suitcase, and in his arms he held a large mattress covered in grey cloth. He is like Mr Hakeem, Isaac thought – in white clothes and white hat – a dark bushy beard, far thicker than Papa's pointed one.

'Come with me, please. I will show you the floor space, you can put down your things, then you can wash. Down the hall is the lavatory,' Mama said and she led him into Isaac's room, shut the door.

A hammer was being struck against his heart. Heroic strength was needed not to shout, 'Go away, thief,' and Isaac bit on his lower lip. After a few minutes, the man came out and went down the hall.

Before going back into her bedroom, his mother turned to him, 'Minnie and I have to finish sewing the dress tonight, so after washing, you go to bed. Mr Saleem helps his cousin carry the fruit crates, so he gets up very early. It's light outside, you can read for a little.'

He put his dish in the sink.

'Good night,' Mr Saleem said as he passed him.

Isaac made the straw in his mattress crackle as he tried to find a comfortable place to read. He couldn't stop moving, itching, scratching – there were always the bugs that escaped. Also, from the mattress next to him came a harsh smell that burnt his nose and stopped his concentration. The gagging smell from Mr Saleem continued to smother him, even though the window was open, letting in the heavy street air. Sweat under his arms, between his legs, but in the story in the far away Yukon, it was icy cold with shining pure white snow extending to the far horizon. What a wonderful thing it was to be a strong man, free to find one's own way in life. To face danger, be brave, recognise a friend and welcome him. He plunged into his book.

Thornton couldn't hold on any longer. Then he saw the dog coming and as Buck struck him with the whole force of the water's current, he reached up and closed with both arms around the shaggy neck. Onshore, Hans snubbed the rope around the tree. Struggling, suffocating, dragging over, Thornton...

'Isaac. Isaac.'

He broke through the swirling water; up from the racing river and saw his mother in nightgown and shawl waiting by the door.

'It will be hard for Mr Saleem to sleep with you making noise reading. He has come far, is tired.'

'Not yet, Mama. I'm at a very exciting moment. Please.'

She came over, bent down and took the book. 'Tomorrow you'll read.' Then with an apologetic gesture, she closed the door behind her.

To be told he mustn't read about bravery and loyalty! Hot anger poured through his body, he clenched his fists. But, wait, wait, Mama wasn't free either. It wasn't her fault they needed money. That was the truth. It was all so hard not to be angry, not to speak out.

Looking through the window he saw the summer light, heard voices shouting from the street. He faced the man's back with its white shirt, bumpy shoulders, brown arm. Mr Saleem was breathing heavily; Isaac didn't want to watch his ribs move and closed his eyes.

From his parents' room on the other side of the wall, he heard his brother David talking, laughing his high boy laugh, and there was Annie saying funny words only she understood. He missed David. Just because he was the oldest son he had to lie here beside a man who smelled and snored, while life with the family went on without him. It wasn't fair. I will earn money when I'm older, he vowed, not sell floor space.

Sticks of straw were poking through the cover, scratching his back, making him squirm. He rolled up his nightshirt a little, lifted it to make a breeze and moved his legs, wriggled his feet. But there was something – something pricking his toe, some sharp straw. He lifted his head.

Pointed claws were clinging to his foot. His scream filled the room. 'Rat! Rat! Mama!'

'Allah, Allah!'

'Mama!'

The rat was running up his bare leg, over his knee and he violently threw himself off the pallet. Squealing, the rat scurried over the floor, climbed up and over his hand and was heading for his orange crate.

'Ich com. Ich com,' his mother was calling, and holding a broom she rushed in. 'Wo ist's? Wo ist's?'

'My foot, my leg,' he cried, holding on to her as he tried to get up.

The man pointed.

In the twilight, Isaac saw the grey rat scrambling up his wooden orange crate, climbing onto his precious folder. Now, standing on hind legs, it was waving its claws, then dropped squealing as it dodged behind his books. His mother swung the broom, the crate cracked, splitting pieces of wood, scattering books, his folder, and the rat dropped.

'My books!'

The rat was running along the skirting board and his mother tried to hit it again. Shrieking, it fled up the peeling wall, climbed to the ledge under the open window, and darted over it.

Breathless, his mother was bending over him. 'Did he bite you?' Carefully she ran her hand over his pale skin, the thin branch of his leg, but there were no teeth marks. 'We are lucky, he didn't have dinner from you,' and trying to laugh she rushed over to the window and closed it.

Mr Saleem stood up tall and thin in his long white shirt. 'I rent space, pay money. First night, rat.'

She was looking at him, searching for words to tie together. 'Mr Saleem, you from India, I, a Jew from Russia. God above knows we both wish there were no rats in Jubilee Street. Rubbish sits in the streets here. A window open, a rat comes. I am sorry ...' She went over to Isaac, touched his hair.

Mr Saleem kept looking at the slivers of crate on the floor. 'Three days I am here from Srinagar. Many trams, gas lights. My cousin sells fruit. Great London has rats. Tonight we keep window closed,' he said.

'Then, no air.' She went over to Isaac's scattered books, the folder, gathered them together, put them beside him. 'They are safe. Now, sleep.'

He reached for her hand. 'Mama, please don't worry. You know there were three kinds of rats in Whitechapel and the

Docks: brown, grey and black. In 1665, the black ones brought the plague.'

'Enough. It's over. Tomorrow, school.' Taking the broom, she left.

The sharp pointed claws still seemed to cling to his foot. He shook it again, and his stomach heaved. No cover to protect him, too hot and he wiped his wet face. But it won't come again tonight, he told himself. Mr Saleem turned away from him, restless.

Tomorrow he would fix his crate, order his things perfectly. He would draw a new picture of a brown man in a long white shirt and white hat, show it to Mr Usherwood. More important, he had decided to write a few special words in his folder, speak of what he read and saw around him, including fear, aloneness and a moment of unexpected joy.

Isaac Rosenberg, poet, artist, 1890-1918.

Highbury Fields, *a sentimental tale*

Rush. Rush. Saturday was even worse than the weekday race to work, the evening dash to her course at Birkbeck College. Today she'd miraculously got Clare and Sarah out of bed and off to their Boots Saturday jobs, re-filled the larder at Morrison's and finally picked up the dry cleaning, having left it with Mrs Tang at Steam Cleaning two months ago. Now she deposited the clothes in the living-room, then quickly ordered the kitchen before her rarely seen, but dear friend Janet arrived for coffee. No one had time for chats now and this was such a treat that Sally didn't want to miss a single second. There was so much to tell.

After kisses and hugs, she urged Janet to sit down and set two mugs of coffee and a plate of biscuits on the kitchen table. Sitting opposite, Sally tried to control the wobble in her voice as she began, 'Paul said he wants all our pots and pans to take with him. I don't know why he's so vindictive – he left me.'

Janet's round face melted in sympathy. 'Yes, dear, that's typical. You'll see, he'll want everything. But what did the judge decide?' she asked, taking a quick sip of coffee.

'We have to go to court again because Paul won't compromise about the child support and he wants to sell our house.' Sally looked lovingly at the unevenly plastered walls, the pine Welsh dresser with its selection of blue Spode china, the ormolu clock perched on the very top shelf – once Islington style. A lump in her throat, but she forced herself on, 'Paul also says he wants me to give up my child psychology degree course, to get a full-time job.' After saying that, she had to turn away to wipe the tears.

Janet shook her head. 'You're studying, and assisting at school three days a week. What else does he want?'

'It's not enough, he says,' and shivering, Sally pulled her old Marks & Spencer cardigan tightly around her.

Janet frowned. 'What a bastard.'

For the hundredth time, Sally let her mind re-run the recent nightmare of watching Paul stand in front of the judge. Abjectly, he'd explained that he moved to Paris for his work, and now was living in a single room. With moist eyes and trembling lips he confessed that for a month he'd not had a job, and now money was short.

Sitting in court Sally wanted to scream, 'Liar'. She ached to list the gifts Paul had bought bloody Françoise – the Paris flat, jewellery from Asprey's, clothes from expensive shops in London and Paris. Luckily, her clever solicitor had sleuthed that Paul was on temporary leave from his job in Paris and was pretending to be unemployed to avoid paying the Highbury mortgage. But if the judge swallowed Paul's lie, she would lose their home. The possibility was so terrifying that only her solicitor's warning to be silent, made her sit in court with both hands clamped over her mouth.

Janet leaned over. 'What does your solicitor need to do?'

Sally wiped her eyes again. 'She has to prove he's not broke. But she can't do anything without dated receipts showing that Paul has recently been spending money on Françoise. Without those, the judge won't listen. Either I keep quiet or I must find evidence that Paul was lying. Without proof, he can sell the house.'

Janet put down the empty coffee mug. 'Darling, I'm so sorry. And how are you and the girls coping with this awful situation?'

'I keep explaining that Paul really loves them, that it's just me he doesn't want. But Clare and Sarah still feel rejected.' Her nose stung as she blew it. 'He's full of hate about everything. Said he can't stand families. Then why does he have another?' She bit her lower lip, then blurted out 'Françoise has had his child. We're replaced. The girls are distraught.'

Pushing her chair closer, Janet put her arms around Sally, 'Oh, God, how shitty people can be.'

Sally nodded and head to head they sat in silence for a long while. But when the clock chimed twelve, Janet sighed. 'Dear, it's time. I'm so sorry, but I have to dash. First, it's Waitrose, then the twins will be back home from Ealing Drama Club at two and starving.'

'Clare and Sarah are both working today, they'll be back later this afternoon.'

'That's great. I'm really happy that my two are enjoying their first-year sixth form,' Janet said, picking up her handbag.

'Clare was too, until … Sarah still has her GCSEs to do. I only hope that Paul's leaving won't undermine them,' and she pushed herself up. 'Thanks so much for coming. I'm sorry I'm such a bore.'

'Oh, no, no don't ever think that,' Janet said, with a hug. 'See you soon, Sweetie. Things will be better. Spring is on the way.'

Sally sighed, shut the door and returned to the kitchen – hers and Paul's. Years ago, she'd taken a sledgehammer and knocked down the dividing wall to make the room larger. He'd said that without an RSJ the ceiling would collapse, but it hadn't. So, they'd worked together, she plastering and painting the walls, and he building all the cupboards. In their eighteen years together they'd had their two girls – shiny bright Clare, Sarah, her bubbly drama queen. Sally sighed, pushed back the curl that had fallen in her eye.

It was when she was assisting at Blackstock Infants that Paul, who was brilliant at languages, was headhunted by an international company based in Europe. So he'd moved away, worked and lived most weeks in Paris, successfully selling assets from businesses that failed, and returning home at weekends. But the longer he spent away from London, the less he understood what was happening in Highbury. Recently, his tongue became sharper, his concern about the family less.

The cruellest moment came at their very last family lunch. Clare and Sarah had witnessed her cringe when Paul belittled their once shared enjoyment of books by attacking her college course. With his mouth full of duck à l'orange, he said, 'Reading deflects you from success in business. Psychological probing is a bourgeois crutch that leads nowhere.' A pained silence followed for the rest of the meal, and after Paul left she'd not seen him for weeks.

One Saturday afternoon their good friend, Martin, dropped by for a drink. 'In Paris recently,' he said. 'Paul has moved into a great flat in the 14th, facing the Champs de Mars. One of those Art Nouveau buildings.'

Sally was pouring the wine. 'Really? He'd not mentioned moving.'

Martin took the glass. 'Well, I don't know how to tell you this, but I think you should know,' and he took a large drink. 'Now that there are three, they need more room.'

She splashed a red pool on the table.

'Françoise looks very well. A rather skinny baby though, lots of black hair. His name's Gilbert, I think.'

'Françoise...' Sally lost her breath.

'You remember her at the Paris office – tall like you, but a well-upholstered blonde. Close for years. I'm surprised she wanted a baby, but there he is.'

Sally managed to stay standing. Martin's eyes were looking at her and she understood. 'Traitor,' she shouted. 'Get out!' He quickly swallowed his wine, grabbed his coat and ran. She collapsed into a chair and was there when Clare and Sarah came home from school. Telling them, they all cried together as if Paul had died.

After a few weeks, Clare and Sarah were able to cry less. They still were upset, but they began to sleep again. For Sally it was different. Each night, drenched in sweat, she lay screaming into her pillow. Each day she taught, studied child behaviour, kept house, comforted Clare and Sarah, and offered them a happy outlook for tomorrow. Over the months she forced herself to take one step after another away from Paul, until she'd arrived at today's bloody battlefield for the house in Highbury.

Saying goodbye to Janet left Sally drained. Studying might help, but before starting she had to clear up, put away the dry cleaning. Off came the plastic on her cleaned raincoat and on Paul's old jacket, to be sold on eBay. Holding up his wool jacket, her cheek rubbed against the lapel's softness. Oh God, the pain, the pulsing desire that rushed through her body. 'No, no do not ever want him again,' she cried and ran to the hall to thrust the jacket into the back of the cubby-hole. It was then that she saw a brown envelope sticking out of the pocket with her name in Mrs Tang's writing. Opening it, she shook out the contents: twenty Euro, a French garage receipt for Paul's Mercedes, two tags, a plastic card – Paul's diamond store card for *Reine of London*. Ready to throw the tags away, she stopped to read: Thai silk dress. One thousand seven hundred and eighty pounds. Mock fur jacket, two thousand four hundred and fifty pounds, *Reine of London*, South Moulton Street.

Sally felt sick. Looking down at her M & S cardigan, she whispered, 'So much money spent on Françoise! How could he!' Holding the credit card, the tags, she stumbled upstairs and dropped down on her bed.

Eyes closed, she sank into oblivion. In her mind's eye she saw a giant Paul without any clothes on. His greased blonde hair sticking up in the air, his hairy arms curved around his huge pink belly. His large prick was jutting in and out like a goose's neck and, as he strode alongside a line of naked women, he took a poke at each one of them. Nearby a giraffe, with a pink hair-ribbon on each of her soft horns, stood watching. Her mouth tried to make a sound, but failed. Instead, Sally-giraffe tottered over to the women, but as she came close each naked woman stuck out her tongue to sound a loud raspberry.

'Stop it! No more insults,' Sally cried, sitting up. And that was when she looked again at the things in her hand shouting, 'You must get a receipt. You have the price tags, his card. Did he recently buy the dress at *Reine*'s? Fight! Fight for yourself!'

She crawled out of bed, and holding onto the cupboard door opened it, took out and put on a long black skirt, a black top. After tying her old Hermès scarf around her neck, she looked closely at her reflection, 'Remember, Sally, The fault lies not in our stars, But in ourselves, that we are assholes.' Her blue eyes glittered as she put the card and the tags in her handbag.

At the top of Highbury Hill there was a taxi. 'Fifty-six South Moulton Street, please,' and entered the first cab she'd been in for eighteen years. Sitting on the edge of the seat in the dark interior, she opened her handbag to review the tags that showed over four thousand pounds spent on bloody presents. Her forty-third birthday was next month and what sort of gift would she be getting? Zero! All at once a glorious aurora borealis of an idea illuminated her mind. Why not buy a shining dress for herself at *Reine*'s? Why not use Paul's card to pay for it? A gut laugh exploded.

The cab went past Selfridges, around Grosvenor Square, then down South Moulton and stopped at an eighteenth-century brick house where a polished brass sign announced, *Reine of London*. Confidently Sally paid, then stepped out onto the sunny street.

A window by the entrance enticed her over and there, framed in gold, was a portrait of Madame Reine. On her jacket, woven from rainbow ribbons of silk, glittered a fist-size diamond brooch. A magnet pulled her closer to Madame Reine. A thin nose, bobbed hair, a light smile on her not-young red lips and Sally felt her knowing black eyes pierce straight into hers. In that look, Sally felt herself shrink to nothing. Again she was the grotesque giraffe, an idiot to have come. Aware that it was futile to deal with a woman like Madame Reine, she went to signal a taxi.

'Good day, Madame,' called a voice. Sally turned. The friendly voice continued, 'How may I help you?'

She looked for the CCTV. Of course she needed help, help to keep her house, look after her girls, and with a deep breath Sally answered, 'I'm Mrs Paul Watersmarsh.'

'How nice to see you, Mrs. Watersmarsh.' Then, 'Madame, do you have an appointment?'

Remembering the receipts, words gushed out, 'Do excuse

me for not phoning for an appointment, but I was away at the showing in Milan. Not finding what I wanted, I returned unexpectedly to London to look for a gown for my birthday celebration.' What a load, she thought, but no questions came and that allowed more lies to flow. She cajoled the voice, asked to see Madame Reine's 'New Line', and even mentioned Paul Watermarsh's recent purchases. And Sesame, the door swung open!

Standing opposite was a young woman in a one-piece tight black top and slim white trousers, her eyes smiling a welcome. 'I'm Leanne. We are so pleased to meet Madame Watersmarsh,' she said and, after looking at Paul's store card, showed her to the lift.

Stepping out, Sally breathed in the delicious 'Mont Blanc' perfume. She stopped to look around the salon and it seemed as if she had walked into a play – entered a large stage filled with fantastic globes of light, exotic plants, huge mirrors. There were vibrant coloured chairs and settees that divided the space into scenes – in one, a tall model performed in an exquisite, side-buttoned black suit, and in another, a slim model moved by wearing a clinging silver gown.

Leanne led Sally to a chair. 'You have not been here before, I believe?'

'No, this is my first visit.'

'I will send a model over and we'll see if together we may find the perfect birthday gown. Of course, I'll inform Madame Reine that you are here. Would you like something … a glass of champagne, wine, coffee?'

'No, no thank you,' said Sally and watched Leanne leave the stage. This play will soon be over, she judged, as she followed the models showing their dramatic outfits to the women seated nearby. Her confidence was slipping away – never would she be able to convince anyone that she was like Françoise. Her earth-brown fingers would betray her even before she started to ask about a receipt.

A tall model came over wearing a long black silk jersey dress; the material plunged low between her breasts. 'Beautiful, but no thank you,' Sally said. And there was Leanne holding up a coral gown for the first Mrs Watersmarsh to see.

'I can ask one of the girls to wear this, but you should try it on. You will see this is perfect for your tall, slender figure. Please, feel it.' And Leanne let the delicate chiffon caress Sally's hand. 'Madame Watersmarsh, your friends will admire you when they see you in this gown. I believe this is right for you. Please come with me,' and she led the way out of the salon.

Following, Sally found she was in a blue fitting room, mirrors surrounding her, plaster cherubs peering down as Leanne helped her out of the old skirt and into the new gown. The silky material moulded to her body, the chiffon flounces falling around her hips. In the mirror she saw the deep plunge of the back set off the warm shade of her skin. How the bright coral was a rich contrast to her brown curly hair with its flashes of grey. For the first time in years she saw herself. Why hadn't Paul told her she could look like this? Why couldn't she appreciate herself? She shut her eyes not to have tears fall on the material.

'What do you think?' Leanne asked. 'I am right, yes?'

'It is lovely.'

'It is lovely on you, Madame!'

A knock and a woman with a pincushion on her wrist entered. In the triple glass, Sally watched the fitter smooth the silk sheath, pinning small tucks to allow the materiel to fit even closer over her hips and breasts.

'It will be perfect,' the fitter smiled. 'How splendid to have a figure like yours – tall and slim. A beautiful woman. D'accord, ma petite Leanne?'

'Oui, Madame Rose. I see you approve too, Madame Watersmarsh. We can have the dress ready next Thursday, all right?'

'Yes, thank you.'

They took away the dress. And alone in her bra and pants, Sally saw the mirror's illusion of 'beautiful' had gone – she was skin and bones. What a ridiculous thing she was doing, out of anger and frustration tricking Paul into buying a ball-gown she would never use. She didn't even know how much it was. And yet ... Wasn't it wonderful to be beautiful for even a moment? She looked at herself again, ran her fingers through her hair. Why not be selfish and grab the moment at Paul's expense!

She dressed and found Leanne waiting outside. 'Please come with me. Madame Reine is looking forward to receiving you in her office.'

The game is up, her heart thumped. She followed Leanne and went through a wide door to pass a busy outer office, enter into a large room where Madame Reine was seated wearing her silk jacket, her diamond brooch. She rose from behind her desk, came towards Sally, her arms open wide.

'Madame Watersmarsh, je suis ravie à faire …'

She didn't hear the rest as Madame's arms held her firmly. Then Sally gently stepped away. 'Madame Reine, I, too, am delighted to meet you. Please forgive me, but my French is poor …'

Madame's pencilled eyebrows went up, 'But I thought …'

'Once I spoke French, but now sadly it's gone …' Sally looked into the searching eyes, 'I do want to tell you, Madame Reine, that the dress and jacket Paul bought recently were very much appreciated. And the new gown is beautiful, just right for my birthday.'

'Ah, Madame, c'est gentil. Please sit down,' and Madame Reine reached for her glasses. 'Where do you want the gown delivered – the new flat in Paris?'

Discovery was near, she must end the interview. 'Oh no, Madame, the ball will be in London…' and reaching for a pen, she quickly wrote her address. 'I forgot to ask how much the dress is?'

Madame Reine picked up the paper, looked at it. 'Yes, Islington is charming… Two thousand, eight hundred and seventy-five pounds.'

Sally's mouth was dry as she unzipped the side pocket of her handbag, took out Paul's card and handed it to her. Then, taking a deep breath she said, 'Madame, I wonder if I could have a dated copy of the receipt for the dress and jacket Paul recently bought … It will be needed for tax purposes.'

Madam Reine was busy with the card. 'Until next month, we are old-fashioned, you will have to sign for your husband. Here.'

It was done. 'The dated receipt?' Sally reminded.

'Mais oui,' and Madame spoke into the intercom, then turned. 'It will be ready in the office in a few minutes. How is your husband? A man of charm. Is he also in London?'

'He is very busy in Paris. Hopefully, he'll be in London soon,' she said, getting up. 'I'll look forward to next Thursday and the delivery. Thank you very much, Madame Reine,' and again the arms were about her.

Madame Reine stepped back, studied Sally for a minute. 'Chère Madame, may your birthday be a happy beginning.' Then at the door, 'Au revoir, Madame Watersmarsh. Bon courage.'

Sally's face flushed. 'Thank you, Madame Reine.'

Waiting in the office seemed endless until she was given the envelope. Sally took Leanne's cool hand, then got into the lift.

But it was hard not to open the envelope. She walked fast past the American Embassy until she was near Selfridges. Her fingers were trembling as she lifted the lip, unfolded the receipt for the dress and jacket, saw the date … A lump in her throat. She must tell her wonderful solicitor. Fumbling in her bag, she found her phone.

'Bravo, Sally! Congratulations! The house in Highbury will be safe,' her solicitor said, then laughing, 'Why not go back to Madame Reine's and have that champagne?'

The precious envelope went back in her handbag. Sally looked at her watch ... already twenty past four. Time to get the Underground. 'I'll walk through Highbury Fields, see the spring daffodils,' she announced to the passers by.

A Jazzy Evening in Old New York

Jazz – Charlie Parker, Ella Fitzgerald, Dizzy Gillespie, the great Louis A – Oh God! So when Jimmy, my roommate's father, called up last week and said that he was coming to New York and that he'd take Nina and me to 52nd Street, the Music Box, to hear Sarah Vaughan and Eddie Duchin, well, I almost screamed. But life is never simple. The night before Jimmy was due in from Toledo, where he now lives and works as the top ladies coat buyer for Macy*s Toledo, (the greatest store in the world); Nina called him to say she wasn't free. Her boyfriend had just surprised her with theatre tickets, and Nina wanted to go with him. Sorry, Dad.

No Sarah Vaughan. I was totally desolate. My face dissolved. I ran to the bathroom.

'Laura, give me a minute,' Nina called.

I despaired. The first and last time I'd have a chance to go to the Music Box. As a freshman at New York University, none of the guys I knew had any money. I blew my nose.

Nina opened the door, smiling. 'I've done it. Dad wants you to come with him, without me. You're to meet him at 9.00 p.m. at the Music Box. He says he's a second dad, known you since we were ten.'

I gave her a big hug. When Jimmy lived in New York, he always made me laugh, twisting words to make funny meanings. After all, he was a graduate of City College of

New York, the poor boy's Harvard. Now I was to go with him to hear Sarah Vaughan!

It was important to look right for 52nd Street, so in new three-inch heels, a long black skirt, a frilly white blouse, I took the Subway from our room in Brooklyn to that amazing street. The cracked maroon canopy over the Music Box welcomed me, but there was no Jimmy. Five minutes later I caught on – I had to open the magic door myself and just go in.

Inside, the walls were painted black. At the bottom of the stairs a large, smoky room was crowded with tables, waiters shouting orders, men and women pushing by me in a hurry to sit down. Then I saw the centre of attention was at the far end of the room, at the edge of the busy dance floor. There, caught in a spotlight was a small, curly-haired man playing drums. Eddie Duchin, bent double, was filigreeing the drums with his sticks, dropping into a brushed whisper, then tattooing the drums to a wild crescendo. Inside my body I went drumming with him.

'Laura!' With smoke seemingly pouring from his ears, there was Jimmy standing, conducting me in his direction. I followed, dodging the closely-knit dancers, the waiters carrying drinks, until I got to his table.

'I'm sorry I'm late,' I said with relief, sitting down next to him in the dark alcove. My face was dripping hot. I was glad a partition separated us from the next table.

'It's fine. Five minutes until the main show begins,' and Jimmy gave my arm a friendly pat. A halo of scotch encircled him. 'How about a drink?' He waved at the black waiter. 'Another round,' and took my hands in his. Looking closely at me he said, 'Isn't this fun?' For no reason he began to laugh, his bow tie bobbing up and down. I couldn't help myself and together we rocked with laughter. 'I love you like I love Nina,' he said, and we laughed some more.

We danced and I managed very well in my high heels. He didn't want to talk about Toledo or his new job at Macy*s, so we didn't speak very much; it was the music that carried us. But there was no sign of food, only a semicircle of glasses that covered the table, and more scotch kept arriving.

A sudden drum roll, house lights dimmed.

'Ladies and Gentlemen, the one and only Sarah Vaughan!' Everyone shouted.

Into the centre of the spotlight walked a light-skinned black woman wearing a pink satin dress with waves of flounces that flooded the floor. Her brown hair was formed into sticks, held in place by grease. She wore bright red lipstick on her enormous mouth. I couldn't believe ugliness like that.

She began to sing. Her dark voice reaching up high, covering octaves, and holding the different notes until they were full, then slowly letting them go – some mellow, some so unbearably hard that they cut into me. She bent over, writhing, painfully pulling out the sounds from way deep inside her. All her music was there, and it was being given to me. I couldn't bear it – it was so wonderful.

Glass in his hand, Jimmy lolled over beside me. 'She's great, isn't she?' He paused. 'You're great too.'

The most amazing sounds I'd ever heard. We clapped loudly at the end of her last song and in the darkness Jimmy reached over to touch my upper arm. I smiled at him because I didn't want him to be hurt, then pulled away and enthusiastically began to clap again. The waiter arrived with more scotches.

'Here we are, far away from our boring lives. Isn't that wonderful?' He laughed. 'Sweetheart, I'm going to look after you. You and Nina are my babies.' He raised the glass and drank to us.

The lights were low and so was the music. We listened. Jimmy's skin was pale and his crinkly hair shone wet. 'I'm so lonely,' he said and bent over to bury his face in the frothy lace of my blouse.

'Please.' I tried to wean his heavy head away. My body started to tremble but he stayed planted there. 'Jimmy,' I begged, but his arms encircled me, holding me tight. Wanting air, he lifted his head, placed it close to my face, his head wobbling a little.

'I need you, Laura.' His hand landed heavily on my right breast and began to knead it. For a moment I couldn't believe what he was doing. Then I tore at his scrabbling fingers and pushed him away. He teetered on the leather seat and holding the edge of the table looked at me. I could see him small, as in the wrong end of opera glasses, his bow tie pointing up, lying on the neck of a little pig-baby. The small eyes barely caught the light, but they peered and pleaded with me.

'Please, Laura, I didn't mean anything … Please, please forgive me.'

'Jimmy, please.' I couldn't bear it any longer – the smell of scotch, the club swirling with smoke, Jimmy's cries.

'I have to go now. Sarah Vaughan was wonderful.'

'Five minutes more,' he pleaded.

Shoving though the crowd, stepping on feet, running up the stairs, I burst out of the Music Box door into the cool New York night. Down the street I ran, until I finally reached the Subway and went inside. I saw a Brooklyn train coming, and with a dime I pushed through the turnstile and through the door.

Sarah Vaughan's voice was wrapped around me with all her truth. But I still heard Jimmy's cries. Bending to the pain in her music, I kept on moving with the train.

The Roofer

Andrew always found it hard to get up the morning after he and Miranda returned to their French cottage. They'd arrived late last night from London and it was a pity to leave the warm round comfort of his wife's body, but the beep from the approaching bread van kept insisting that he rise and struggle into his dressing gown. As the sole Englishman in the village of Mont Plaisir, he felt obliged to greet the early morning bread van as the first customer.

Every day, except Tuesday, the van stopped in front of the old mayor's stone house to bring bread to the village. So, accompanied by the bright April sun Andrew crossed the road to exchange greetings in French with Monsieur Bonjean, who was both baker and driver of the van. For one Euro sixty cents Andrew received a handshake, a kind comment about his good health and two delicious baguettes.

Touched by Monsieur Bonjeans' welcome, Andrew headed back home holding his long breads tenderly against his yellow and blue striped dressing gown. Then he saw Madame Chevalier approaching. Of course there was no need for embarrassment about his dressing gown – in all the twelve years he'd been coming to the village he always wore it when buying baguettes. But he prepared himself for her French greeting.

'Bonjour, Monsieur Harris,' and Madame Chevalier's brown eyes drilled into his. "How is noisy, foggy London?"

Gesturing to indicate the plane trees around the boule pitch and then including the entire street, she proclaimed, 'A Mont Plaisir, toujours le calme.'

'True, it's always calm here in Mont Plaisir,' Andrew echoed.

'That is what the village is – calme,' she went on, her head nodding. 'As such it is understandable why Monsieur et Madame Harris come here.'

Andrew found it appropriate to agree with Madame Chevalier, although at times he did try to contradict her observations about the English weather. After a firm handshake and another good day, he started to cross the road towards his cottage, but was immediately distracted by a movement on the church roof. This was unusual and demanded investigation. So hurrying past the morose stone soldier commemorating the two World Wars, he stopped by the church.

The large nineteenth-century red brick church with its cone-shaped tower and steeple was rarely opened for service, so Andrew was puzzled to see a figure standing on its sloping roof. He strained to see, and yes, of course, it was Laurent Maquin, the roofer. The son of the mayor stood perched fifteen metres off the ground, his hat pulled down against the morning sun.

Suddenly, Laurent began to wing his way over the slanting expanse of roof tiles, bending over to replace the grey slates that were broken or missing, darting here and there to check that the new ones exactly overlapped the lower ones. After stopping to review his work, the roofer ducked down the ladder to reappear holding a metal object. He paused on the ridge-tiled backbone of the church to examine the tower, its steeple, then crossed over to begin to climb.

Watching, Andrew felt his hands go weak as Laurent reached for the metal rung above him. Stepping on one rung after another, he pulled himself up higher until he stood at the very top of the tower; his body framed against the blue sky. Now the roofer held up the weathercock he was carrying and delicately placed it on the tip of the steeple. And there the cock stood, tail arched, surveying his land. Then caught by the breeze, the weathercock swung in pride towards the south.

Overwhelmed, Andrew ran to the bread van eager to join the customers in a round of applause, but found Monsieur Bonjean alone busy putting away his money. Crossing to his cottage, he rushed down the hall and into the kitchen calling, 'Miranda, did you see that? Wasn't it a magnificent sight! What daring! My knees were knocking, but Laurent didn't seem afraid at all.'

'Yes, he is wonderful. I saw him from the window,' she said, and to punctuate her enthusiasm reached over to tear off the end of a baguette. 'But I'm also famished.' Chewing hard, she went to fill the coffee jug.

'A courageous man. A man the village can be proud of. How lucky we are to be here,' said Andrew carefully laying down the baguettes, before sitting down at the table.

'True. But we've lost tiles, too. Do you think he'll have time to fix them? It seems to have been a bad storm,' Miranda looked up at the damp patch on the ceiling.

'He knows about it and will drop by later, tell us when he's free.' Cutting the baguette in half, Andrew added butter and jam.

Around him was the sound of crusts being eaten, the bitter smell of French coffee, as Miranda filled the porcelain bowls. A long drink, a sigh and Andrew settled back into his chair. 'After that excitement, I'm looking forward to starting on the garden. The shutters need varnishing, too. Do you think you could have a go?'

'But some time today I have to work on the text of *The Dream*. You've probably forgotten, rehearsals for my school play start in two weeks' said Miranda, twisting off another piece of bread and adding a knot of butter, 'Oh, to hell with my diet, we're only here for six days. Now I'll have the strength to paint,' and munching she got up, went out onto the veranda and down into the garden.

Andrew looked around at the wooden cupboards, the white enamel cooker. Breathing in the friendly kitchen smells made him think of the many breakfasts shared. The times when Tim – bright eyes, wild hair, sat here talking, savouring with him a baguette and coffee. Such pleasures existed when he came on holidays with them. A long time ago now. Well, he had to accept that his son was permanently working in New York, involved in financial matters about which he understood little. Andrew looked out through the double doors at the rabbit shed. Attached to its end wall was the trellis he'd put up ages ago, still holding the promise of summer roses.

During this short break, there'd be enough time to look over the garden – plant more flowers, have a brief escape from the worries of writing the new grant proposal to access funding on Mesopotamian archaeology, on which his future depended. Thirteen years ago was the last time he'd been to Iraq, months spent in Baghdad classifying the Nimrud Ivories. Where were they now? That did not bear thinking of. He put his bowl in the sink, went out onto the veranda.

In the clear April air Miranda was sanding down the shutters. All was not lost he thought, and went into the shed. From its chilly interior he carried out a bag of compost in preparation to dig in the Hellebores Niger and Erysimon Mauvet. He stopped for a moment to look up – over the garden a blue sky. From the magnificent weeping ash tree a thrush was singing.

A shrill interruption, the front doorbell was ringing and Andrew looked at his watch. Time had gone by too quickly, it was almost twelve. Calling to Miranda he went to answer the door.

'Bonjour, Monsieur Harris. I hope I'm not too early?' Laurent was there, his hand held out, the hat in the other.

'Bonjour, Laurent. It's fine,' and Andrew shook his hand, looked into his sun-creased face. 'Come in, please,' and led the way. 'May I offer you an apéritif – a Rafael, or a coffee?'

Laurent smiled, 'A Rafael, please,' and followed Andrew into the kitchen.

It was cool there. He poured out the watery drinks, adding globes of ice, slices of lemon, when Miranda came in holding up her hands. 'Bonjour, Laurent. Excuse me, they're covered in dust,' and after a quick wash, shook his hands.

Andrew put out some nuts and they sat by the table quietly drinking, resting. Streaks of sunlight dappled the room.

Laurent's eyes closed for a minute, then, embarrassed, he opened them. 'Pardon me. Recently I have set out over seventy slates, so my body orders me to shut my eyes,' and he laughed. 'It is exact work. For the church, it must be perfect.' He lifted the slice of lemon from his glass and sucking, grimaced.

'I saw you on the roof with the weathercock … What a splendid job you've done!' Andrew said.

'Because of the bad storm, there were many tiles broken. It has taken me four days to finish. Out in the sun, it is not easy, Monsieur Harris.'

'I can well imagine. But I admire your great skill. Your courage,' and Andrew poured him another drink.

The hard muscle in his arm bulged as Laurent raised his glass, 'A votre santé.' He drank, put it down, and leaning forward spoke quickly. 'I am fifty. I cannot survive doing roofing for five more years – that is when I can retire after working for forty years. Everything costs dear in France, taxes high. Day after day up a ladder in the cold – the summer heat is even worse. My back has suffered. I appear strong but the arthritis is bad.' He moved closer – a cry burst through his words. 'I have not lived. All is work. My wife is not interesting. I have seen nothing.' He shut his mouth, lowered his head.

Andrew looked at Miranda, who was watching the whorl in the wooden floor.

Laurent waited. Then he stood. 'Thank you for the apéritif. You are here until when?'

Andrew cleared his throat. 'Saturday we return.'

'I'll do your roof on Friday afternoon. Now lunch is ready over at my father's. We eat at twelve, en famille.'

'Thank you, Laurent.'

Andrew and Miranda got up, shook his hand. They went with him to the door. As they came back into the garden, Miranda bent down to pick up a small stick and went over to where she'd left a tin of varnish. He watched as she began to stir. After a time he said, 'We have been allowed to hear something important.'

She nodded. 'His despair.'

'Laurent does have family, continuity.'

'Whereas we …'

'In our lives we have been places, seen a thing or two. Enjoyed our work.'

'Yes, but …'

'We come here for the calm,' he reminded her.

Miranda looked at Andrew. 'Now I don't trust the calm. I'm afraid of its underside.'

In the weeping ash, the thrush opened his heart.

Lacrimae

'You don't love me. I'm dying. I'll kill myself!' Outside in the December night Graham tried to blot out the hoarse cries echoing in his head. Suzanne's soap-opera performance, he thought. At the same time he tried to distract himself by waving frantically at the passing taxis, until finally one came to a stop.

'The Tate Gallery. Hurry. Hurry,' and Graham slid onto the seat. Damn her, she's deliberately made me late.

The cabby moved down Half Moon Street, but was stopped by the Piccadilly traffic.

'Hurry, Guv? You must be joking. The week before Christmas!'

'Well, push it as fast as you can. I'm bloody late,' Graham called. With a crescendo of blowing horns, the cabby nipped into the stream of cars.

But he couldn't stop himself arguing with Suzanne's tears. What the hell was wrong with going to a party for Universal Television's top brass? Scotch with the big boys he worked with. Scotch by the statue of the Three Graces. The prospect was exciting, an opportunity to be acknowledged for his success as a producer of their high-rating television plays. She knew how important this party was for his future, so why in God's name should she complain about her small operation? Around his waist, the elastic from his boxer shorts started to itch.

Calm down, Graham told himself, just listen to the words on the cabby's clock. 'Head of Drama. Head of Drama', it clicked. Why shouldn't it happen to him? He was one of three on the short list. Not only was he a West End playwright, but he had experienced a big success with producing Somerset Maugham's stories on TV. Just that extra chatting-up tonight would help. With luck Philimore might still be there, available for a word before the big meeting on Thursday. His shorts were making him writhe in his seat; he must be allergic to the soap powder.

They were passing Piccadilly Circus, golden with Christmas cheer. 1967, a great year, and he smiled at the thought of it. Next came the Houses of Parliament, then the Tate Gallery and Graham sat up. He smoothed down his white hair – fifty and careful blue-white, no tobacco-yellow hair allowed. Oh, the evening could be fun, if it wasn't for Suzanne. I won't worry about her now, he thought, as the cab stopped.

Inside the Tate Gallery, the noise bubbled. After checking his coat, Graham waited for a moment near the great pillars to appraise faces – the enemies, the friends. In the distance a large hand was flapping at him. Of course Toto was watching out for him, always ready to ease his entrance. A friend for thirty years, Tobias was an actor of clergymen, officers and dons. So many memories of working together in the theatre were revived by that wave. Toto, a bird from the past, but one who could fly everywhere and with everyone. He watched the heron approach.

'Graham, hello, and just in time to miss the welcoming speeches. But where is your darling Suzanne?' Tobias looked down from his benevolent height in surprise and wonder.

'You know she doesn't like these parties. Also, she's had a small operation to get rid of the bags under her eyes, and they've done something so she can't stop crying. They'll put it right, I'm sure, but now she's driving everyone crazy with her tears.'

'Poor dear. I shall come over first thing in the morning. Do tell her how wonderful she was on the telly in *The Children*. I saw her in the re-run. The scenes in the ghetto made me cry and cry. But, Graham, you must have a drink, speak to a few people, enjoy yourself. I'm told Christmas is only a week away.'

They walked under the great dome, passed the jewelled Christmas tree. Tobias went over to say hello to friends, and Graham stopped a waiter carrying tumblers filled with scotch, and took one. After a quick drink, he looked around to see if anyone on the short list was still there.

'Graham dear,' came a gentle tap on his back, and he turned. Golden haired Angela stood there, slim and smiling. A terrible actress but always a pleasure to look at, and he happily exchanged kisses.

'Loved your production of *The Kite*. A wonderful series,' she smiled.

'Many thanks. I wasn't sure if they'd come off, but it was great fun to do Maugham. And you?'

'I'm off to Spain on a film about Cortez, the great

Conquistador. They need a token blonde,' she laughed, showing her perfect teeth.

Graham had always appreciated them, marble white against her bright lipstick. 'Cortez had a girlfriend called Marina, they're probably writing her in for you,' he said, smoothing down his hair. But the moment was stolen – from behind the nearby pillar appeared a figure in a beautifully tailored dress suit.

'Good evening, Graham,' an accented voice called.' No flirting, or I shall report you to Suzanne. I'm her loyal spy. Heil Hitler.'

'Heinz! God, everyone's here.' Damn it, queer, all-knowing Heinz was here to watch him, condemn him. Looking into Heinz's unwavering blue eyes, Graham thought he saw Suzanne mirrored there, also judging him. Quickly he turned away. 'You know Angela Moore?'

Heinz bowed over her hand, 'Miss Moore.'

Tobias called over. 'Kissing hands? Dear boy, the age of meritocracy is here. All those roles of European counts and Nazi officers have affected you.' He threw up his hands in mock horror.

'I cut my teeth in old Vienna. I fled from it, but I'm still infected by it.' And Heinz turned to Graham. 'My past is my luggage and bank account. As it is with Suzanne. But we also share a common ill, a black hole where our hearts used to be.' He reached for a passing flute of champagne. 'To you, Miss Moore, and your charming English heart.'

Graham wanted to say something rude, but how could he?

Heinz was Suzanne's best friend. Two ambitious refugees desperate to succeed – for Suzanne, to find love through acting, for Heinz, to make money. Both mistaken.

'I understand Suzanne's not well.'

'Heinz, politics have called me, that's why I'm here tonight,' Graham said, turning away. 'Any sign of the Head, Toto?'

Tobias nodded. 'Philimore is by the statue of the Three Graces with the Director of Programmes. I understand he has to leave soon. And Graham, Julian Silver is here.'

'Suzanne can't get over being fired by him, the bastard. Heinz, please call her tomorrow,' and Graham walked towards the Head, trying to time his arrival with a break in the conversation. Luck came when he saw the Director of Programmes pat Philimore's shoulder, wave, and then join a small clique of friends. He allowed a few beats.

'Good evening, Philimore.'

'Nice to see you, Graham.' He turned to the statue. 'How do you like our three marble ladies?'

Graham weighed his thoughts as he looked over the white unblemished beauty. 'Perfection is difficult for me to appreciate. As a writer, my subject is human foibles.' He took a deep breath, 'Philimore, do you have a moment?'

'Yes, Graham,' and he let his chin rest on his chest.

'I've had a few ideas that I wanted to discuss with you. As we turn towards the end of the century I thought why not dramatise a series of stories by British and American writers. Writers who have sharpened our thinking, our use of language:

Tennessee Williams, Amis, Waugh. If it's all right, I've got an offer to make and will leave it with your secretary?'

Philimore lifted his head, his eyes looking inward. 'Yes. Fine. Thank you, Graham, I'll have a look, let you know.'

A heavy woman in navy silk-taffeta was hovering behind them, and now she cut in. 'Philimore, excuse me for interrupting, but we're going to be late. We must go now. The car's waiting outside.'

'All right, Molly, I'm coming. Graham, do meet my wife.'

She quickly shook his hand, apologised for their terrible hurry while urging her husband on. Graham felt his ideas were teetering off the shelf as he watched them go.

Across the room, a short stout man smiled at him and he nodded back. At last a positive sign, and from a friend of Philimore's. God, I'm getting superstitious, he thought. A smile's a vote. Oh to be Head of Drama. He looked around again. A wave, a grin, a warm glance to friends, enemies: Robert, Vanessa, Ben, Clive. You never know how the dice will roll. All grist to the mill. Mixed metaphors! At last another scotch came by.

'Take one for me, Graham.'

Whose Manchester voice is that, he wondered and turned, holding the two glasses. A red face crowded close to his, wild grey hair curling in all directions.

'Julian Silver! What brings a famous film director like you to this gathering of TV hacks?' He handed him the glass, avoided touching his fingers.

'Didn't you know, you boys are planning a Retro? I'm not

dead and you're having a season of my films. I'm touched. How's Suzanne?'

'Fine. Working.'

'Glad to hear it. Finished shooting last week. Tell her how sorry I am that she came to Italy for nothing. No one's fault. Derek's forty, looks twenty-five. No sexual electricity between Suzanne and him. And Lola was free, so it all slotted in. It's in the past, anyway.'

Graham watched his Adam's apple moving up and down. 'Of course.'

'Send you an invitation for the Première. Probably a Royal Performance with the Queen. Good to see you, Graham.' He smiled and, waving to someone in the distance, walked away

Bastard. Graham emptied his glass. Suzanne's pale face flashed in front of him on the day she'd been fired. 'My last big chance lost,' she had cried. Of course that wasn't so, he told her again and again, but he remembered noticing her thin body, the lines under her eyes. For a woman nearing forty, finding parts was always difficult. Graham reached for another scotch. Realistically speaking, Silver was right. The past was over. One must move on. Today was all. He knew this was his moment to step onto the highest rung as a successful producer, a writer, a man without illusions. He would not fail. Someone behind him called his name. Shut up, he thought, and waited before turning.

'Ted Arnold,' the young man announced. 'I'm a writer. A friend of Suzanne's.' He put out his hand. 'You and I met recently at a story conference. If you'd done another series of Maugham's stories, I was scheduled for it,' he laughed.

Graham took his hand. He remembered – Cambridge, a bright spark. 'Yes. Sorry.'

'Your wife was also in the film I wrote, *The Children*, just re-run.'

Graham felt energy filling the space between them. 'Yes. Of course. A fine film. What a pity it wasn't a big-screen success. An exciting script, acting, direction. We were so disappointed.'

'The scenes in the Theresienstadt ghetto with Suzanne and the children were so moving. We all love her. It was an unforgettable time working with her. Is she here?'

'No, she's a little under the weather.'

'I'm sorry. Do tell her it's something of a cult film now, she might like that. Also send love from Ted Arnold.' He reached for Graham's hand and shook it hard. 'I'm off. Happy New Year to you and Suzanne.'

Graham watched the young man walk away and inside his head heard Suzanne scream. It had started again.

The first night he had heard her, he'd screamed too. On the other side of the bed her dark figure sat plucking at the blankets, talking, screaming. He had called to her again and again, tried to break into the terrible dream by putting his arms around her, but the endless cries in German continued. He had got to know her dream, once loved her for it.

LACRIMAE

She is standing in the street in her nightie, with Pappi's jacket on, holding tight to Mutti's hand. Looking up, she watches the men in brown uniforms upstairs in her bedroom. The windows are open wide as the little blue chair is lifted, broken against the wall. She won't cry, just holds tighter to Mutti. Pages from her books float down. A man is holding her dear doll Karen – her blonde head is pulled from her body and thrown from the window. Falling, Karen's head turns, her blue eyes look at her. She hits the pavement. Suzanne screams.

For years the dream had repeated itself to her, to him. It had become a record in his head. He took a deep drink, another. Oh, God, where was Toto now? He looked around at the people, their voices chatting, laughing. Stop. Look. The satin-dressed women, the Savile Row men, he knew the time was right for him to be like them, to enjoy the luxury and pleasure of success. He had had enough of memories. Ten years with Suzanne searching for a comfort he could not give, recognition of her work that did not happen, it was enough. Now that he was near the top of the ladder, he would decide that her past wasn't his any longer, that her searching blue eyes, her thin body meant nothing to him. He would speak to Tobias now, find encouragement.

Graham looked around at the crowd and saw his friend standing near an enormous painting of the Holy Family. How strange that Toto, who had never married, would be able to play the role of Saint Joseph. He quickly walked towards him and passing a tray, took a refill.

'Had a nice talk with the Head? A fine man,' said Toto warmly smiling.

'Brief, positive, to the point,' and Graham took a drink. 'Anything new with you?'

'Both Heinz and I are in a film together. He's a high-ranking Nazi officer and I'm a high-ranking British officer. The script we don't know, but we can guess,' and he laughed.

'Any important people still here?'

'Undoubtedly you've nodded to the main ones. The others on the short list have made the rounds and gone.'

'Where's Angela?'

'Last seen talking to an important director. Over there,' Tobias gestured. 'She'll be back.'

'I must speak to you.' Graham felt angry and his waistband had begun to itch again. 'Suzanne's had an operation, which she thinks affected her lacrymal gland. She's crying all the time, can't stop. She's hysterical – saying that I don't give a damn. She wanted to have the operation done, thought it would get rid of the bags under her eyes, help her looks, get work. She threatened suicide if I went to this party. Frankly, she doesn't want me to succeed; she wants me to fail.' He was burning. 'It is true, Toto, I don't give a damn anymore.'

'Old man, take it easy. Maybe this lacrymal thing is serious. Graham, you're doing well. It's not easy for her now. She's helped you so much, the beautiful home she's made for you, the entertaining. People love her.'

'That's in the past. Now she's threatening suicide to blackmail me. Wait, Angela's coming over. I'll call you tomorrow.' He saw her moving towards them, the director in tow, the yellow satin dress catching the light as she walked.

'Graham, meet Larry Rossi, my favourite director. Graham Turner. I believe you know Tobias.'

'Of course. Good to meet you, Graham. I enjoyed your television series very much.' He pumped his hand.

Graham surmised: forty, divorced, New York-Italian, now California, and smiling said, 'Thanks, Larry. Now I'm involved in a new project – a dramatisation of a series of American and English short stories: Tennessee Williams, Waugh, Amis.'

'Sounds interesting. We're just off for a meal at The Ivy, would you and Tobias care to join us?'

'Do come.' Angela's fingers touched his.

'Just for half an hour.'

Tobias took Graham's arm and they walked to the coat check.

The Ivy was a pleasant blur. Angela was sitting next to him in the booth, enfolding him in her Chanel No. 5, while in his hand a scotch on the rocks tinkled.

'I understand from Tobias that you're married to Suzanne Carlisle. Seen her act often, a favourite actress of mine.' Larry picked up Angela's hand, turned it over and began to trace the lines. 'She was wonderful on TV recently, about the Czech ghetto. Did she have first-hand experience with the Nazis?' He looked up for a minute.

Graham felt the elastic on his shorts itch again, saw the California tan, the little eyes. 'She may have.'

Larry smoothed Angela's palm. 'I see Spain calling. A great success. And there's a man!'

'That's what everyone reads; it's almost predictable,' she laughed and, picking up her glass, turned to Graham. 'Shall we drink to good fortune – ambition rewarded in 1968?'

'Good wishes from friends are always welcome.' He touched her glass and drank. It went to his head. He looked down at Angela's golden hair and Graham suddenly needed to feel the silk of it, to touch her face, her throat, the deep crease between her white breasts. For ages he'd wanted nothing, only to finish the next programme and to escape from home. He smiled, feeling her thigh brush his. He also felt Suzanne's presence. She had no place here, and in defiance he turned to the three, letting words blurt out unexpectedly. 'All of us here, I believe, are beginning a new journey in our lives. Am I right?'

'How extraordinary you should say that,' Tobias said quietly. 'I hadn't the courage to tell you …' He stopped.

Graham looked at him, saw he was blushing. 'Toto, do tell us about your planned journey; we promise we'll guard your secret.'

Tobias pulled his long body together, looked at them. 'I'm sixty-seven. I'm getting married, for the first time.' He let out a light laugh. 'Jane is pregnant … Yes, it's my child.' He sat still, his bright eyes looking at Graham. 'I'm very happy. Old friend, what do you say?'

Graham's stomach turned. What a thing to do! He looked at Toto's grey hair, his eyes with the swollen puff below the eyebrows. Horse face. But what a kind man, a good brain, read Classics, a minimal actor though. But so loved. Now going out of his life. Having a baby. How dare he at sixty-seven think he could be a father. At fifty Graham knew he was too old. He took a drink, ordered himself to smile.

'How wonderful, Toto,' he said. 'I think you and Jane will be very happy. What a wonderful surprise.'

Graham got up, went to Tobias, shook his hand. He wanted to vomit at the enthusiastic chorus of 'Congratulations', but instead caught the waiter's eye and ordered another round.

'Graham, don't tell Suzanne tonight. We'll be around tomorrow about eleven to tell her. Jane's play is closing in a month, we'll get married then.'

'Fine. Perhaps you can cheer Suzanne up, she's convinced her career's over.' Graham turned to the others. 'Something about her tear duct being injured; she keeps crying all the time. It'll be all right, of course, but I'm accused of a lack of loyalty.' He picked up his glass. 'My turn to toast – to Tobias and Jane.' The bitter taste made him shut his mouth.

Tobias put his hand on Graham's arm. 'Thank you, old friend. I hope the Head of Drama will be yours, that all will turn out well.'

The room was beginning to turn; there was a knocking in his head. Graham breathed deeply, swayed slightly. 'I must go now. A Happy Holiday to you all.' He bent over and kissed Angela's hair, turned away quickly to wave his hand at the rest. The room was tilting, but fortunately he was helped on with his coat, the door opened.

Outside in the cold he stopped swaying and waited as the doorman tried to flag down a taxi in the half-rain, half-snow. Shivering with the sharp change, Graham watched the other late-night people caught in the same anxiety of leaving one place to journey to the unknown next. Finally a cab and he climbed in.

'A mixed bag of an evening,' he said aloud, not caring what the cabby thought. He gave himself a 'pass' mark for politicking at the Tate. The party had been worth going to. Damn it, Suzanne had no reason to threaten him. Also people thought well of her work. He'd tell her that, if she behaved decently. Then Angela's face came to him, her cool, quiet, ordered person. How wonderful to be part of her stable world. The nervous itching around his waist troubled him. He must be calm, and looked out at the falling sleet as the cab cut through the night.

The front door into the Green Street flats thudded shut and Graham waited by the cage for the lift to descend. A sixty-watt bulb made a black shadow far up the marble stairs and from the top of the building he heard the distant sound of the moving chains. Not Marley's Ghost, Graham reassured himself. On the house committee he had voted to keep the old-fashioned lift as part of the period flats, but tonight he was sorry. In the creaking half-dark he suddenly felt unsure of everything – the future, even the past, especially how to treat Suzanne. Hopefully, she would be asleep.

At the fourth floor, the lift clanged to a halt. He got out, waited, then opened the door to his flat. A wave of hot air hit him. She had pushed up the thermostat to baking. The hall light was off, and only iced moonlight came through the living-room window. She had forgotten to put the night-lights on, so he would have to proceed to their bedroom by finding the lights as he went along.

Suddenly a terrible need to pee swept over him; he was dizzy with the urgency. Holding onto the wall he felt his way down the hall in the dark in search of the toilet. The aligned pictures swung on their hooks and grasping one it fell onto the carpet and he heard the crunch as he stepped on it. But he couldn't stop and went on, dancing to keep in the pee. At last he felt the crystal knob to the loo door, pushed it open, flicked on the switch, but the light blinded his eyes and he had to squeeze them together. Through the slit he saw the toilet seat's open mouth and rushed to it. Total ecstasy as he torrented into the bowl and at last shook off the final drops. He was filled with huge pride as he watched his yellow frothy river swirl away.

She had tried to make him feel small, unimportant, like herself. Other women knew he was someone, appreciated him. Tomorrow he would speak to Suzanne. Tonight he needed sleep. He opened the medicine chest, and enjoyed the cool drink of water as he swallowed the last of her Librium. Tomorrow he would remind her to call the doctor for more. Damn, the elastic was itching again.

'Get rid of these goddamn clothes,' he shouted, dropping his trousers, pulling down the boxer shorts. He felt a burst of joy at scratch, scratch, scratching his waist, the hair on his crotch. He pulled off his shoes, and with a kick he floored everything under the sink. Free! Free from ten years of marriage! Suzanne's understanding was no longer important, nor her lovemaking. There would be even more beautiful homes than this, and women, when he arrived at the destination he wanted. Now he was going to her, but the truth was he didn't need her.

He shut the light in the loo and stepped out. Standing in the warm hall without clothes on, he felt strong. The darkness rested his eyes and he felt his head was steadier. The flat he knew perfectly, but as he walked on the soft carpet his head began turning again and he lost his sense of direction. Shadowy things loomed upside down and he found he wasn't sure where he was. A table was in the wrong place and, pushing against it, the china pieces cracked into each other. Hearing himself shout for lights, he reached out to where they should have been and hit his thigh against a barricade of furniture. 'God damn you,' he cried, then covered his mouth.

Limping on through the dark he breathed the familiar smell of Suzanne's body and he knew he had reached their bedroom. Exhausted, Graham stood by the open door trying to see inside, catch some light through the drawn curtains. He heard the silence, the air barely moving. For no reason his heart beat faster and for a moment he was tempted to call her, as he often did when he came home late. But he thought about what he had gone through, the memory of her swollen eyes. Tomorrow would be soon enough. Stepping carefully, he crossed to his side of the bed. His pyjamas had been folded as usual and placed on his pillow. He put them on, then lifted the covers and got in. Thank heavens, he thought. The pillow held his unsteady head, and he began to relax, breathe more easily. He stretched out his legs, inadvertently touching her cold foot. Graham looked over at his wife's still figure. Suzanne must be feeling better now she's asleep. I'm glad I didn't disturb her.

Hungarian Teeth

'Malcolm Lewis – on the Hungarian Teeth Package.' Automatically, his tongue felt for the cracked remains of Upper Left 2 and 3, Upper Right 3 and Lower Right 5, as he waited to be welcomed to Hotel Wolfgang, Budapest.

The receptionist ran through the reservations and announced in a hard, sharp voice, 'All people here are for teeth. Room 303. Sign. Key. Breakfast seven to nine. Lift.' Undoubtedly a rude descendant from old Communist days, Malcolm decided and defiantly scribbled his name, grabbed the key, his suitcase.

A lady whose white roots shone through her dyed black hair was standing by the lift, holding a handkerchief over her mouth. Looking apologetically at Malcolm, she said in a Dublin accent, 'I'm sorry, young man, but I've just come from the dentist. Two teeth removed.'

What candour, he thought. 'I hope it's not too painful. I'm also here for the dentist.' And as if to underline their mutual ordeal, the lift clanked its arrival and together they rocked upwards.

Again speaking through her hanky, the woman announced 'It's my second trip. The first – three teeth out. Next time an imprint for the bridges. Thanks be, I'll be going home tomorrow,' and she dabbed the blood off the edge of her lip. With a sudden jerk the lift halted and the door opened. 'Good

Luck, dear,' she said smiling, and Malcolm saw the wide empty spaces.

Seeing no teeth made his stomach turn, bringing up his recent British Airway's chicken wrap. He swallowed hard, clamped his mouth shut while the lift rose again. Oh God, how he hated dentists – men sent on earth to torture the defenceless. He hadn't been for ... was it now twenty-two years? The nightmare of his teeth being pulled still haunted him.

Ten years old with four teeth cracked from a down-hill fall from his bike. And there he was sitting in the tilted dentist chair, when all of a sudden the red-faced dentist placed a rubber thing over his mouth and nose, told him to breathe deeply. He tried to call out to his mum in the waiting room, but the rubber cup muffled the words. Then, a thick dozy feeling swamped over him; the ceiling above circled and he felt himself sliding down a giant's throat ...

He remembered how difficult it was to open his eyes. When he finally did, a different man, a strange man with glasses was bending over him. His mum's white face was near. 'An anaesthetic overdose,' he heard the man say. 'Your mum brought you to hospital just in time.' Malcolm looked into her watery blue eyes.

Afterwards, when his mum tried to drag him to a dentist he bit and kicked, shrieked that she wanted to kill him and that he'd never, ever go to a dentist again. Finally, she gave up. But twenty-two years on, when every cold and hot drink made his teeth vibrate with pain, what could he do? It was only because of sweet Lucy that he recently decided to face his fears and see a dentist. Not a cold, red-faced, greedy English dentist, but rather find a kind, inexpensive one. Perhaps in a lost-in-time country like Hungary, he just might be able to overcome his terror.

Arriving at the hotel's top floor Malcolm stepped out of the lift, took a deep breath and rolled his suitcase down the hall. In room 303 he found a monk's cell with a narrow metal bed, a small TV on a small table, and a dormer window looking out onto a busy crossroad. The constant movement of traffic outside caused reverberations in the confined space, making his teeth ache. Should he go home? No, no, he mustn't be put off by crude circumstances, but remember that the Hungarian Teeth Package was displacing the greedy private English dentists.

A cacophony of beeping horns sounded in the street and Malcolm poked his head out of the window. Below, a crush of cars was expelling clouds of grey smoke as they passed an ancient bus that had stopped to pick up passengers. There was also the smell of something burning. Not the bus he realised, but across the street a women in a long black dress was cooking bits of meat over a charcoal fire, and passers-by were stopping to eat. How artless Budapest appeared in comparison to his sophisticated life in Islington.

Each day he taught English at Blackstock Boys' Comprehensive, (always following the syllabus), then after the last bell he'd pop into the 'Old Cock' pub for a beer and a chat to replenish his spirits. Lucy, assisting at the infant's school up the road, usually joined him to sweeten his day. Two years ago, when they began to discuss their future together, there was the real possibility of buying their own two-up, two-down in Tower Hamlets, but that was before the crash. When they recently spoke about their plans it was Lucy who started to object, and her brutal frankness shook him. If they seriously shared, she'd said, he must accept she didn't want children, and that watching him brush his awful teeth every day was a deal breaker. Hearing that, his heart shrivelled … No children? A dentist, or no Lucy? He'd said nothing, just looked at Lucy – her thin nose, her round pouty mouth, her long baby blonde hair, her delicious perky breasts. So he came up with this decision: if his future depended on new teeth, he'd agree to a dentist. As for children, he still assumed they'd have two, but that wasn't really important now. 'Okay, seeing a dentist will be a bridge to our future,' and he'd laughed with his mouth shut.

Eleven o'clock, his watch was telling him to take his first trip to the dreaded D. With a hand wet with fear Malcolm locked the door and rode down to the lobby. He told the receptionist to order a taxi and was soon deposited in front of the dentist's address, no doubt once a beautiful Art Nouveau building, now pitted and grey.

He found Dr Imrè Nagy's name listed, his office on the top floor. After pressing the buzzer, he managed to push the heavy wooden door open and began to climb flight after flight of dirty marble steps. Huffing, puffing, Malcolm stopped at the top landing to order his greased hair, catch his breath and, as he looked up, he saw white clouds in a blue sky. Incredible – he was standing on a balcony open to the heavens and overlooking an interior square filled with broken discarded furniture. As he turned to face the door to the dentist's office, cracked Upper Left 5 throbbed.

But inside was a miracle – newly painted walls, shiny equipment – everything in order. A plump Dr Nagy greeted him, his English careful and minimal. Inviting him to sit in the chair, the dentist gently prodded around the upper and lower teeth, took X-rays. Quietly he advised Malcolm, 'Not worry. Have good time, return tomorrow nine o'clock. But if you decide not come, Mr Lewis, you call. Have good day.'

In the street Malcolm was elated. Black terror had been momentarily lifted, encouraged by Dr N's teeth discussion. Tomorrow only three teeth needed to be pulled, four filled … a mere bagatelle! Yet and yet, should he? Yes, Lucy would be proud of him; a brave man prepared to suffer for his first full smile in twenty-two years! Now he deserved to be rewarded with zest-filled food, a sprinkle of culture and after riffling through *The Rough Guide*, he headed towards the appropriately named Heroes' Square.

The Square was full of bronze statues of brawny, mighty men, and seeing their shiny muscles bulging next to his meagre ones, Malcolm decided to give them a miss. But the art museum was opposite – a Greek-pillared building, and upon entering he felt relaxed, especially when he found the coffee shop. His stomach was growling with hunger, and as all the tables were taken he decided to be a friendly tourist and share. Balancing his sandwich and coffee, Malcolm nodded to the two ladies who were finishing their lunch and sat down opposite them.

At last a reward for battling fear – he bit into his first Hungarian salami sandwich, then slowly, slowly sipped the creamy latté. The sweet peppery salami was delicious and he leaned back relaxed and able to coolly take in the two women sitting across from him.

It appeared the grey-haired lady was leaving, addressing the waitress in Hungarian, but not a single word could he understand. Then, turning to her friend, the woman explained something to her in English. That was when he really saw the younger woman – a pale face, framed by a halo of red-gold hair. He was marvelling at the Titian colour when he caught a lilting Dublin accent in her answer to the woman's 'goodbye'. What a delightful coincidence, another member of the dentist brigade and he leaned over. 'Please excuse me, but you must be here for your teeth too,' and he offered half a smile.

'Pardon?'

'Hungarian dentists. I've just been to a very competent one. I'd recommend him. The other lady from Dublin had two teeth out today and is fine. I'll have three out tomorrow.' But seeing the woman's fair eyebrows shoot up, Malcolm stopped. 'Upsetting? I'm sorry.'

'Excuse me, I'm a docent, not a dentist …'

'Oh!'

'I take English-speaking tourists around the museum and explain the paintings to them,' she said firmly.

'Yes. Of course. I'm very sorry,' and feeling his face turning red, Malcolm studied his coffee cup.

The woman turned away to write something in her notebook. It was the sun filtering through her wondrous hair that filled him with the desire to try again. He spoke humbly, as if to an Ofsted examiner, 'Excuse me, Miss Docent, are you still taking ignorant people around the museum today?'

She looked up. 'Of course, if there are any waiting. El Greco is the painter today.'

'I'm not so familiar with his work.'

'There's a special exhibition of El Greco. A fast-living Greek artist, who lived and painted in Toledo, Spain.'

And this was how he met Katie Burgess, who was spending three weeks visiting a friend, the vice-consul at the Irish Consulate, now assigned to Budapest for three years. But after seeing sights for a week she'd decided that being an English-speaking docent on sixteenth and seventeenth century Spanish paintings was what she preferred doing. He learned this during the tour when, as the sole English visitor, he was guided and lectured to on El Greco's original way of creating elongated figures. Together they examined his enraptured figures that, by using his expressive technique and brilliant colours, allowed him to be way ahead of his time. Unfortunately, those in power in Spain remained unimpressed.

After in-depth studies of cardinals, several pièta, scenes of storms in Toledo, Katie Burgess's voice became a little hoarse. It was then that Malcolm apologised for interrupting. 'Excuse me, Miss Burgess, but aren't you a little tired? Please don't think I'm rude or unappreciative, but perhaps we might leave El Greco and go for a cool drink somewhere? I'd like to see more of the city before the dentist begins his bloody work tomorrow. Today, may I suggest, we play truant for a very short while?'

Her eyes narrowed to examine him. At last, 'Being cliché Irish, I think a drink might suit.' Katie led and he followed, descending stairs then turning to the main entrance.

First a Metro ride, and then he was led into a large open square surrounded by elegant shops. 'This is rather like an imitation Paris. Tourists keen only to shop or sit in posh cafés eating cake,' he complained. Katie said nothing, so he continued to follow her as she walked on.

It was then he stopped. In the centre of the square stood a tall, dark-haired woman. She had begun to sing – her strong true voice filling the square with an intricate and dissonant melody. As he listened, the music sang of a passion and pain that was also rooted within him. He became part of the song, the aching melody carrying him away, filling him with loss and hope. Katie called but he stood there. She called again and he stumbled over to the singer, mumbled something, offered money.

'Wonderful,' Katie said. 'Weren't we fortunate to hear this!' Then looking at her watch, 'I'm so sorry, but I must be home by six. Come.'

He followed. The woman's song stayed with him as he was led to the far corner of the square. He was brought to a café and given a glass of red wine. Seating opposite Katie, he wanted to say something about this extraordinary moment, but there were no words.

She was watching him, waiting, then shaking her head said, 'Oh Lord, what on earth am I doing here with a silent man? Under his youthful hairstyle no comments exist about the wonders he's seen and heard. His only concerns are about teeth extractions and fillings. I must be off my rocker coming here.'

Malcolm leaned forward, his heart banging so loud he could hear it. 'Katie Burgess, try to understand. I am a humble teacher of English Language and Lit in a London secondary school – to describe the woman's singing, the music's meaning to me – only poetry by John Keats could do that.'

She covered her mouth with her hand.

Her narrow shoulders in the thin blue blouse, her vulnerability gave him courage to go on, 'About painting I can offer something because I know little. I will admit El Greco is fine, but give me Kandinsky any other day – his imagination, the colourful objects colliding …'

In a soft voice, 'Yes, yes. You have true answers, Malcolm,' and Katie took a quick drink. 'These artists create the shapes of profound expression.'

'Yes,' he said, now dabbing his face with the serviette. 'I can't top that … But I need a moment to recover. I'm not used to such things. Please, let us return to simple matters,' and he took a drink. 'Nice wine. We're agreed I'm a social disappointment, but why then did you come?'

'It's so mundane that you'll smile.'

'Can't.'

But she did, showing straight white teeth. 'I'm here to take a break from the ordinariness of my single life. Nothing for you to hang on to there. Have you children?'

'No. Lucy doesn't want any.'

She ran her fingers through her hair, burnished gold. 'My kids are wonderful, but sometimes difficult. Bernadette is thirteen, Karen, twelve. They are in an International Camp in Budapest and angry with me for making them come here in their holiday to see a different life. They want to be at home with their friends … To decide to stay, marry again, is my big decision.' She stopped. 'But why am I telling you that?'

He was pleased by her question, but refused to answer. 'Whatever your reason, I want to thank you for coming and for introducing me to all this,' and he looked towards the square.

Perhaps her candour was due to his being a recognisable type – British, bad teeth, a comfort in a strange country. But what a lucky bastard he was to be here. Would Lucy understand his desire to stay in the moment? Appreciate the marvels he'd found today?

She leaned over, 'Malcolm, I hope you're not having fantasies … you don't really do it for me. I'm not the pick-up type anyway, boringly conventional, a follower of strict bonds. I'm here to decide about my fiancé, Paul.' Her worry made a furrow between her bright eyes.

'You know, you don't do it for me either. I'm here for the dentist. To enjoy the wine and to value these heart-shaking moments.' Raising his glass, he said, 'To passing travellers,' and Malcolm smiled at Katie.

Lou-Lou's History of Money

The day Lou-Lou began to understand the word money, was the first morning in all her seven years when she awoke to hear her mommy's high heels go click, clicking past her bedroom door. She sat up, pulled aside the rosebud curtains and looked out of her bedroom window – first up to the blue-black sky, then down to 5th Avenue, where the street lights were still on. Way at the back entrance of her apartment house the garbage men were shouting to each other, banging the garbage cans. This early her mommy wasn't asleep. Why not? So Lou-Lou got up.

Her mommy was sitting in the kitchen drinking a cup of coffee, but without her daddy. She was dressed in her next best black dress, hair done with beautiful waves, lips cupid-bow red and around her neck she was wearing the going-out little foxy-face fur piece.

'Good morning, baby,' her mommy said, sending a kiss. 'I'm so sorry I woke you, but I got up very early today. Things are changing at home, sweetheart.'

Lou-Lou drew back. Was it because she'd done something like – not eat her spinach two times? But her mommy was smiling. 'Don't worry, darling. I'm just going back to work today, to the same job, at the same company where I worked before you were born. Daddy was going to tell you later on in the morning,' she said. Having finished her coffee, she left a lipstick kiss on the cup.

Lou-Lou's mouth trembled, so she went over and sat on her mommy's lap. She let her hold her so tight that the little foxy-fur face with its staring yellow eyes looked into hers. Questions sprang into her head: Who would take her to school today? Meet her at the gate in the afternoon and at home play the radio, sing and dance to *The music goes up and down, oh,oh,oh*, if mommy wasn't there? Lou-Lou shook her head hard, then felt her mommy's soft hand smooth down her curls.

'Please don't be upset, darling. Daddy will be home more often now. He'll be here with you.' Then, looking into Lou-Lou's eyes, her mommy said, 'My big girl, I'm returning to work because it's important to have money.'

But inside, she puzzled over why her daddy wasn't at his office looking over the beautiful designs he made of coats and suits. He always liked bringing drawings home and smiled when mommy went 'ah', as she touched the soft woollen cloth he planned to use. Yet today, instead of going downtown he went with her to school, and called for her at three o'clock.

Day after day her daddy held her hand crossing the streets, and she got used to his prickly goodbye kiss, the hug against his soft coat. When spring came she enjoyed playing tag during recess, running around the one tree in the playground. There were lots of bright green leaves on it now and that meant Public School Six would soon be closing for summer vacation.

But there was no more dancing at home and every day ended the same. After her bath and a story, mommy and daddy would kiss her goodnight and go inside to their big bedroom, close the door and begin to talk. At first Lou-Lou didn't pay attention, but often before falling asleep she'd hear loud sharp words. One night she got up and listened at the door and it was then she heard her mother say, 'It's your fault, Philip. You're a failure.'

Then her daddy shouted, 'For God's sake, can't you understand anything, Joanie! No orders are coming in. There's no money.'

'Others are selling. Lo Balbo is on top. You must be out of touch.'

'No one's buying. I've called the banks; they can't give us any more credit. God help me, the business is going under and I don't know what to do.'

Then she heard her daddy start to cry and her mommy say, 'Philip, stop it. Stop it.'

Lou-Lou had never heard such sounds. She ran back to her room, crawled under the blankets all the way to the bottom of the bed, pushing her face into the mattress. In the morning her mommy found her and told Lou-Lou that she and daddy were sorry if she'd been kept awake. A few days later Lou-Lou was sent to summer camp.

After a month away swimming, doing pottery and singing 'Hiawatha Camp, echoing voices sing', camp was finally over and she was brought home. She was dropped off at her apartment and found her dad was in the living room talking on the phone. His voice was hoarse, like when he had a bad cold and he was saying, 'It's gone. It's finished. God help me.' He hung up the receiver and without 'hello sweetheart,' he went into the big bedroom and shut the door. She stood there and cried. But she understood – her mom was getting money, her dad wasn't.

There were the usual kisses that night, the door closed, and she got up to listen. Her mother had a new voice. 'What are you going to do, Philip?' it asked. 'You've lost the business. I'll see to it that you won't be declared a bankrupt, but you're not able to take any responsibility for Lou and me any more. You must know, I can't stand what is happening to us.'

Back in bed Lou-Lou went over the word 'responsibility'– the first part was okay, but putting the 'ibility' part together she couldn't make out. And 'bankrupt'- she sounded it over and over until she fell asleep. In the morning her father woke her. He was dressed in his office blue suit, a white hanky spilling from his pocket, his soft grey hat on his head, and he was holding a suitcase.

Sitting on her bed he told her in his fun voice, 'I'm going away. I won't be living here anymore, darling. But I'll see you often. Remember, sweetie, I love you.' As he leaned over to kiss her, she looked into his brown eyes and saw awful things there. He got up quickly and began to sing the song she loved, 'Lou-Lou baby, you're the cream in my coffee. You're the cherry in my pie', and holding the suitcase went out the front door.

Soon her mother came in, her cheeks were wet, her red lips pulled together. She sat down and ran her fingers, with their long red fingernails, through Lou-Lou's hair and whispered, 'Darling, don't be upset, everything will be all right. Soon you'll go away to boarding school. You'll leave dirty New York City behind, and the girls and boys there will be your new friends. At weekend visits, you and I will be together. Your father will also visit you at your new school and you'll have lots of fun.'

At boarding school, Lou-Lou lived in a clapboard house with open windows, while nearby different kinds of trees waved their branches in the wind. In class 4A, she found there were big numbers in her Arithmetic Book. Adding up the pictures of pennies, five cents, ten cents, twenty-five cents was fun in the beginning, but after a few days Lou-Lou understood the coins were meaningless. She agreed with her new friend Stanley that the paper coins would be worthless forever. She saw that here at Happy Hills School no one seemed to have real money.

Only on alternate Sundays were there coins and bills. Her funny dad or her pretty mom took turns to drive up and take her for a chocolate-chip ice-cream soda at Howard Johnson's Restaurant. It was there she saw real silver coins and green bills go into a huge cash register machine with a beautiful silver design on it. The drawer lay open, then it snapped shut making the money disappear. But where did it go? And how to get more, Lou-Lou wondered.

Of course her mom knew how to make money, but her dad didn't. After the machine swallowed the last green dollar, Lou-Lou knew visiting time was over and it was time to be driven back to where she lived with the other boarders. Arriving at the house there was a kiss 'goodbye' against her dad's whiskers, or a hug surrounded by her mom's fur coat. Then Lou-Lou would wave, as dad's borrowed or mom's rented car was driven down the road towards the City.

Today her friend Stanley was watching. He was wearing dungarees and standing on the swing that was roped to the branch of a tree. After the car left, Lou-Lou went to sit on the swing, and together she and Stanley began to pump, up and up. She pumped until she could almost touch the clouds with her sneakers, and it was then she remembered the click, click of her mother's shoes. Yes, it was that morning it had all begun. She took in a deep breath of the white air and let out the sound that was held in prison inside. She took another breath, screamed again. The sounds moved the clouds, uncovering the sun. In the warmth, she let go of her father's kiss, her mother's hug.

They were still moving when Lou-Lou said, 'Stanley, did you know some people stop loving when there's no money?'

He nodded, swinging.

A Part to Play

Chorlton-cum-Hardy, near Manchester. Even after four weeks living there, Ann loved its sound of special importance. It was only a short bus ride from there to The Exchange – so she added that name to all the other towns she'd stayed in over her acting years. There'd been many theatres, starting with the Pier at Bournemouth, Dundee Rep, The Crucible, New Vic, Hackney Empire and, oh dear, others she'd now forgotten. A jobbing actor, she'd played so many parts, from Agatha Christie to Gertrude, Hamlet's mother. Yet somehow she had missed Manchester. Now she was here for eight weeks.

Today she'd come to Broughton Park searching for signs of spring, but the yellow and purple crocus seemed slow in coming. Walking by the mums on the park benches, she listened to the open-nosed voices talking about babies. She loved the local melody, and took time to register it in her accent bank before moving on. To listen to people and look at nature chimed together, filled her daytime life.

She watched the shrieking gulls fly over the grey water as they struggled to alight on the island in the middle of the man-made lake. The busy March wind flung her hair about too, but she didn't care. What did it matter when you were in your sixties, no need now to be spring-pretty on stage! Yet it would be a treat if the clouds did scatter for a moment to permit the shy Manchester sun to shine. So, she waited patiently by the lake until the sky did open, allowing a single shaft of light to fall near her. Holding onto the cold railing, she looked down into the golden water.

The magic moment seemed to reflect the birth of the play. Last night's opening performance had been warmly received, and playing her part a growing pleasure. But today she was no longer bound by the smoky community of rehearsals – until the half-hour before the show began she would be creating her own structure. Leaning far over the rail, she saw her face in the water – round, snub nose, bottle-blonde hair to hide the grey – actor. The small waves rippled lightly over her face.

'You're not thinking of jumping in, are you?' A young man's thin face intruded itself alongside hers. 'It's not deep enough.'

A shocking opening line, she thought. 'No,' she answered, but she felt that wasn't enough. 'Thank you for asking,' then edged away.

'A friend of mine tried. They took him to hospital for a few days.'

'I'm sorry.'

'Yass,' he said in his Manchester voice. 'Now he's in a crap hostel. Depression, the doctor calls it.'

Surreal. But damp fear moved across her back. Memories of intruders in her own life – people wanting, men asking for what she couldn't give. She didn't need this, and looked around for a way to leave. As she turned she saw the young man clearly. Tall, bone-thin, short hair, a long nose, wearing a pilot's jacket, the brown leather peeling off like skin.

'Can't his parents help?' she asked.

'You're old. They're old. They don't want to know.'

Ann looked at her watch. 'Well, I hope things will …'

She was interrupted as the pilot shook out a fistful of coins from his pocket saying, 'You're from the South. Lonely. I can manage a cuppa tea.'

'Thanks, but I've just had one. I thought I'd have a walk now. Bye.' She waved in a friendly way, and turning quickly followed the railing around the lake, leaving the young man behind with his change. 'I always feel guilty when I do that,' she said aloud. 'How droll. He thought I need help whereas he … Oh, God, you can't win.'

After leaving a distance between them, Ann stopped to look far out at the island in the lake. She reassured herself, remembering how by following the rules carefully she'd survived in a difficult profession. 'I've made a living, can't ask for more,' she said and smiled at last night's curtain call. She loved to act, glowed in the warm appreciation of the audience, and she did a little dancing two-step. Heigh-ho! Her control wasn't what it once was, but not to worry.

Her father had always encouraged her. Edward loved to listen to her recite Wordsworth, de la Mare, Frost. School prizes, scholarship at sixteen to the Royal Academy. And on the island in front of her she saw her family home in Kentish Town, as in a black and white film.

There were the dark walls of the rented flat where she and her parents lived during her childhood and growing-up years. Her mother, at the kitchen table, listing the 'dos and don'ts' over the porridge. 'No strangers, no foreigners,' Clara always said. 'No one invited to the flat, home immediately after school or a performance.' She could still hear the warning, 'Ann, remember that men always want something. Remember, I'd rather scrub the floor than do 'it'.' Her mother repeated that from eight to eighteen, and more often after she'd brought her best friend home for tea one Sunday. Her Peter, shy off stage, but incandescent on.

Of course life was unpredictable, boring, often frightening. But on the stage was where you lived a varied, a controlled and interesting life. The writer might kill you off in the second act, but it was clear why and how it happened. Real life had no plot, no order – for example, a strange young man might speak to you. So, pretending to tidy her hair, Ann turned to see what had happened to him, and fortunately the pilot had vanished.

Following the edge of the lake, she left the adults and the playing children behind, letting the rippling water lead her to the rocks at the far end. The moving clouds had extinguished the ray of light, so that when she reached the end of the lake the landscape was a silent grey.

The pilot was there. Fear grabbed her, freezing her hands. She saw he had deliberately followed her, with no one to witness. Her only wild hope was that she might shatter the silence, if she had to scream.

'It's deeper at this end,' he said. 'It's better here, few people.'

Ann pulled her coat around her. 'What are you going to do?'

'I don't know yet.'

Looking down at the water, she took a deep breath, 'What do you want?'

'I want to die.'

In her mind Gertrude's words, *There with fantastic garlands did she come. Of crowflowers. Nettles, daisies, and long purples...But our cold maids do deadmen's fingers call them.*

'No,' she said.

'There's nothing.'

In the silence the water lapped against the rocks.

'Please.' She should say more, but knew there was no room inside her heart for others. Her working self, that was the only difference, that was what separated her from him. Life and Death. But she forced herself, 'What's your name?'

'John.'

'Ann.'

'I'm sick.'

Oh, God, what am I to do, she thought? She didn't want to hear, be responsible for him. Please no memories now of her own past, how loss had almost drowned her. 'I'm sorry, John,' she whispered, looking at his young-old face with his closed eyes. She didn't really care, that was the truth. Only to keep herself was enough, not someone else's lost boy. She knew at the end of this act there wouldn't be any laughs or tears, only more of the same.

'I'm here, John, working. We could meet sometimes and talk. That's all I have. I've no money.'

Under his lids his eyes moved back and forth, then he opened them halfway to look at her. 'Why did you turn me down for a cuppa tea? I wasn't interested in raping you.'

Under his cowed appearance, she felt his threat. 'I thought – who in God's name are you to invite me?' She stopped.

'Always insults. Bloody stuck-up old bag. Fuck you,' he said and walked away.

'You fuck off! I don't want anything from you either, or anyone,' she hurled the words after him.

She gasped for air. He went on walking and she thought, good, that's over, finished. But now she was shaking. She'd admitted her lifetime truth, but it hadn't mattered. Instead, her crude words had contributed to his death. She began to cry.

Hiding her face, Ann followed the path behind the rocks that led towards the entrance. But her legs were weak. A bench and she sat down. On stage was where you wept, not in life. She could have hit herself wasting tears that were of no use. Peter's face came, his memory filled her head, her breasts, and he was there. Her dear, dear friend Peter. His young face. Dark eyes looking at her, loving, wanting. Dearest, darling Peter. She reached out, almost touching his hair, his lips. Then from the grave her mother's voice, 'I'd rather scrub the floor than do 'it'.'

Tears ran through her fingers. Somewhere on the bench was her handbag. She searched for a tissue, pressed it over her mouth. Again she covered her face. Footsteps were coming down the path. She lowered her head, tried to make herself invisible.

The person stopped. A Manchester voice said, 'You're crying for me. Yass?'

Through the blur Ann saw the pilot, nodded.

Aim High

The panting blue-black muzzle was next to Hildi's face. 'Beau, stop jumping on me. Cousin Carole and Georges are coming, but you must wait.' She lifted the poodle's paws off her chest, set them down and looked at the three other wriggling dogs. 'Now be good babies. Yes, the visitors are late. I'm going down to watch for them.' At that the dogs folded their black haunches, while their eight eyes continued to follow Hildi as she straightened her dress. After rubbing each head, she opened the kitchen door, closed it behind her.

Halfway down the shared driveway she stopped to admire her Spanish-style house. How romantic it looked in the afternoon sun with its outside balcony, as if pretty señoritas would shortly appear and wave to passers-by. What a fine first impression of Santa Monica it will give Cousin Carole after living in Rheims, she thought.

Watching the cars pass down Hacienda Avenue, Hildi remembered the first letter in years she'd received from her cousin. It came out of the blue, and in flowery words said how much Carole missed her American family, even though she'd lived many years in France. That she hadn't seen Hildi for thirty years, but her mother's death last year had made her keenly aware of time passing. Then she wrote, *'May my husband Georges and I come to visit you? I have warm memories of you and of my Cousin Ted. Please let us try to build a bridge over the time lost; this is very important to me.'*

Hildi read the letter often and came to the conclusion that a bridge like that might be a godsend for Ted. It might answer a lot of problems. So, she decided to invite her to California for her son's sake, and also for the unbreakable tie she felt for Carole's mother, her special Aunt Helena.

The jewelled memory of that long ago summer spent with Aunt Helena made Hacienda Avenue vanish. Again she saw herself at Kennedy Airport waving goodbye to her parents, sitting on a plane for the first time and flying off to Cannes to help look after her little cousin Carole. On her twentieth birthday she saw the Mediterranean for the first time, and there waiting for her by the turquoise sea were Carole and her beautiful Aunt Helena.

The wonders of Cannes were opened to her that summer – the bowing welcome at the Carlton Hotel, the dinners tasting of wine, the delicious flaming desserts. Yet the most exciting times of all were the glowing evening strolls along the Croisette with Aunt Helena. In her perfect Chanel suit, her diamonds and rubies sparkling around her neck, her fingers, all the beautiful people admired her. 'Aim high, Hildi! Aim for the riches in life,' her aunt kept saying, as they walked together in the soft sea air. Hildi promised her she would. Oh, what a summer that had been!

It vanished with her return to New York and to her parent's fried-onion-smelling apartment on Amsterdam Avenue. But she kept thinking about Aunt Helena as she rode the subway, when she got off at 34th Street, and during the endless hours selling ladies' dresses at Macy*s. Even after she married Arthur and moved to Southern California for his job at Lockheed's, then the baby's birth, she still heard the important words.

Every day when she cleaned, washed and cooked, she wove stories for Teddy about the turquoise sea, the magic hotel, and Aunt Helena's starlight diamonds. Describing her holiday as he grew up, she induced him to 'Aim high,' urged him on after Arthur's unexpected stroke – after his passing. Then she found the stories offered a sustaining dream for her loneliness. Now Ted and the memories allowed her to face Hacienda Avenue and the vital question she must ask her cousin. But the rented car wasn't here; it was clear that Carole and her husband were lost on the freeway.

At the kitchen door, the dogs barked their eager welcome. 'Sorry babies, the visitors haven't arrived yet. Now it's time for your run,' and opening the gate she let the dogs riot into the back garden. She shut the gate behind them and upon turning saw a large woman walking up the drive carrying a suitcase. She was at least size eighteen, with short bottle-blonde hair. Was this Cousin Carole? No resemblance to her mother with her dark hair – always slim until the day she died.

'Cousin Hildi?'

'Carole! Is it you?' Hildi couldn't catch her breath, 'Sorry for my hoarse voice.'

'Dear Hildi. I'm sorry I'm late.'

She saw tears in Carole's eyes. 'It's okay. Forget it.'

'This is an important moment for me. We've not met for far too long,' and Carole put her arms around her, bent over to kiss both cheeks.

Engulfed in her cousin's embrace, Hildi realised how small she'd become. She freed herself. 'Yes, thirty years ago. I was visiting family in New York with Ted, he was just a boy.'

'I remember it so clearly. We met in Central Park, the Carousel. Ted and I rode on white horses and he won the golden ring!' As she spoke, it was clear that Carole's voice was caught between laughter and tears. 'I often think about that day. Ted – a wonderful boy. Will I see him now?' Carole's bright eyes looked into Hildi's.

'Where's your husband?'

Carole shook her head. 'Do forgive Georges. It was the end of the semester, and he hadn't finished his work at the University. He teaches 19th century French Literature, but he promised that he'd complete everything in three days, then come.' She took Hildi's hand, held it, 'My dear cousin, his absence gives us time to get to know each other a little, and that's good. I'm sorry to be late, but I was afraid to stop and telephone, afraid of the freeway and being lost. I followed your excellent map, and parked the car on the street,' Carole waved behind her. 'You know my city Rheims is small; even Paris is small compared to your LA. I've lost my big city shoes, I'm afraid,' she laughed.

'Okay. Women without men, that's nothing new, so come in,' but before Hildi opened the kitchen door, she turned to the back garden. 'I've got four large poodles, who mean the world to me. They might jump on you, but they won't hurt,' and with that she pushed open the gate, 'Beau, Fleur, Doll, Cleo!'

The dogs shot out of the garden, leaping on her, their rolling tongues wetting her face and hands. When they jumped on Carole, she tried to push them off.

'Now stop it, Cleo. Down, Beau. House!' Hildi opened the door and her dogs squirmed past, rushing inside. 'They are my babies. Come in,' and as she followed Carole into the kitchen, Hildi saw the pull of her black slacks. Too much French cream, she decided.

Hildi hurried through the kitchen. She knew it told an old fashioned story with its dingy yellow walls, chipped white enamel stove, old fridge. Would Carole's plucked eyebrows go up in surprise at finding no microwave, no central island with electronically controlled knobs? But her cousin said nothing. Was it French politeness that stopped her commenting? Her size, her blonde hair, her silence – Hildi had to figure out how to approach her.

'Please follow me. I'll show you the rest of the house,' and Hildi stepped down into the sunken living room. Avoiding the frayed carpet, she went over to the green dralon-covered couch and chairs.

'I don't use this room much any more. I don't entertain now, but it's a wonderful size. The house is worth over a million dollars now. It's my insurance policy for a place in the old folks' home, 'cause it'll cost a fortune to spend my crazy years there,' and she gave a hoarse laugh.

They entered the TV room, and Hildi leaned against the sideboard. 'Most evenings I sit here watching television. Over there's the doghouse,' she said, pointing to a very large wooden house, a wire gate for a door. 'The dogs are my life, but when one is bad, it goes into the doghouse.' She went over and opened the gate, let it snap shut.

Carole's eyebrows shot up. 'How unusual. I've only ever seen a doghouse in a garden. My daughters, Camille and Antoinette, each have a cat, but I look after them in our apartment. You are fortunate to have such a large house.'

'Yes, plenty of room for the dogs and me. The TV room I use a lot. We'll have a drink here later. Now come along, you must want to wash,' and Hildi started up the stairs.

At the top Beau appeared, tail wagging and poised to spring again. 'Baby, if you don't lie down, you know what will happen!' He turned and padded into a large bedroom, jumped onto a double bed. 'He was a champion, a wonderful dog. When my husband was alive, Beau always slept with us. Now he sleeps here with me. Your room's over there,' said Hildi, crossing the hall and opening the door.

'Two beds still here, for sleepover nights when Ted was young. The pennants over the beds are from his universities, MIT and Harvard. Those pictures on the wall are old photos of the family – aunts, uncles, now gone,' Hildi said, pointing to rows of framed photos. Her face felt hot and she took out a handkerchief from her pocket. 'Now, just a little speech. Carole, I'm glad you're here. Your mother was a great influence on Ted and me. I miss Aunt Helena every day. She knew about life. In her many visits, I spent a lot of time with her. Especially during her last trip to California, when she wasn't feeling so good. I picked her up at her hotel every day, drove her about. But now that she's gone, there are things I need to know from you, to settle my mind. Ted's too.' The handkerchief was damp in her hand. 'But first, the bathroom's here. I'll be in the TV room. Remember, if you don't want dog company, keep the door closed.' Breathless, Hildi turned away to go downstairs.

Going into the kitchen, she lit a cigarette. The time to ask the question was near. Drawing in the smoke, she went over to the fridge, took out the film-wrapped plate of chicken and potato salad she'd prepared for Carole, and put it on the kitchen table. The meal for the dogs was late, and opening a large can of dog food, Hildi laid out the four named bowls. Everything was going well. With a final drag she went to the sink, wet the butt, dropped it into the grinder. Turning around, there was Beau, having finished his dinner he'd started on Fleur's!

'Oh, you bad, bad dog,' Hildi said, catching hold of his collar. He tried to raise his head to lick her face, his mouth was open so wide she could see food on his spotted gums. 'No, no, no, I caught you stealing. Into the doghouse this minute.'

He hesitated, then collapsed. Holding tight, she dragged him across the hall into the TV room. 'Don't you dare cry,' and she pulled him past the sideboard, the sofa, to the doghouse.

Opening the metal gate, she pushed him in. 'The others will eat. You'll stay here,' and the gate banged shut. Heart pounding, Hildi opened the near door to the sideboard and brought out two glasses, a bottle of vodka and tins of tomato juice. Adding ice, she took a deep drink, and there was Carole coming down the stairs.

Hildi cleared her throat. 'Sorry about the noise, but Beau is a bad dog and is in the doghouse. Please, sit down. Is the room all right?'

'Thank you, it's very nice.' Carole said, sinking into the sofa. 'Seeing all those photographs on the wall – the wonderful family pictures, is very moving. There is a particularly lovely one of Mother. How beautiful she looks in her Chanel suit, so elegant. That is how I always like to think of her. As in my childhood in Cannes, when she took us for a holiday. Remember?'

'Helena sparkled like her diamonds.'

'Yes. People always admired her. Hildi, I'm also thrilled to see the pictures from Ted's two graduations, MIT and Harvard, an engineer and lawyer. How proud you must be! Looking through the books on Ted's bedside table, I saw that Harrison Grey's autobiography was signed, "To Ted, my special man." I had no idea that Ted is working for an investment company in New York City. That's wonderful! Do you remember, Aim high? Aim for the riches in life?'

'Yes.' Hildi felt her face burn. 'And your children?'

'Camille, my eldest, is interested in physics and teaches at the same lycée where I teach English. Antoinette is the one who makes money in our family – she works in public relations for the champagne business – as you know, Rheims is the centre.'

'Well, I'm sorry, Carole, but today we don't have any champagne. There is vodka and tomato juice, which is popular here.' Tearing the clip from a can, Hildi poured it in a glass with the vodka and ice, handed it to Carole. She raised her own glass, 'Welcome to the US!'

'To the family,' and Carole took a drink. She swallowed, then waited. 'You know, I've never had this drink before.'

'It's refreshing.' Hildi smiled, and sitting down on the sofa felt the bulk of Carole's body press against her. 'Of course, it's over a year since Aunt Helena's death. You know, I spent a lot of time with your mother just before she returned to New York.'

'I'm so glad,' Carole said quietly. 'It's difficult for me to say this … You may be aware that Mother never approved of my life in France, my marriage, my teaching. Her disappointment was hard for me and for her. So, thank you, Hildi, for being around, helping to fill a daughter's role.'

Hildi's heart swelled as she looked into her cousin's face. 'I was glad to do it. And now that Aunt Helena's gone, her estate settled, I've got to know something. It's important for Ted.' She leaned over, 'Where are your mother's jewels?'

Carole pulled back, then lurched forward, spilling her drink on the floor.

Hildi bit her lip, then cleared her throat. 'I often wonder what happened to Helena's diamonds, her rubies? Perhaps you don't know this but Ted, as her lawyer, started to write your mother's will. Just before finishing, he was told by her to stop. Someone else drew it up. What happened to the cabochon ring, the diamond and ruby necklace, the matching ruby earrings?'

Carole covered her eyes, then took her hand away, 'I don't know. In her will there wasn't any jewellery, only money left to pay bills and a small sum for my daughters. Helena came to visit us in Rheims only twice.' Putting her glass on the floor, Carole took a deep breath, turned to Hildi, 'There wasn't any jewellery. Why are you asking?'

Hildi stood up, 'That can't be true. The diamonds must be somewhere, in some deposit box. She had lots of important pieces.' Her voice scaled higher, scraping her throat. 'They were listed. Ted had almost finished writing Helena's will. She told him to stop. No reason given. Where are the diamonds?'

'Probably she sold them to live. She enjoyed living well. She hadn't worked for years. There weren't any jewels.'

This couldn't be the truth. With a shaking hand, Hildi fished out the pack of Chesterfields.

'Mother's cigarettes. You're smoking the same cigarettes,' Carole whispered.

Hildi lit one. 'Yes, your mother and I agreed on everything. The summer Helena took me to Europe was the most important experience of my life. We shared things, we understood each other. I was her confidante about everything, business, men. Complete trust. She and her jewellery were one. They must be somewhere. Where are they?'

Carole had moved to the farthest edge of the sofa, her arms across her breasts. In the doghouse, Beau was crying.

Hildi looked down at Carole. 'You don't understand about life, the importance of money in America. You lead a simple life in provincial France,' she said, trying to keep her voice steady. 'Your mother was a special person. You never even tried to be like her. After thirty years you come here for a holiday to show your need for family. Aunt Helena was right, you only ever wanted to think of yourself.' She went over to the doghouse, pulled at the gate. 'Enough crying. Out.' Beau scuttled across the floor as Hildi opened the kitchen door, the gate to the garden. She returned, reached for another cigarette, lit it from the first.

Carole was watching. Then she pushed herself out of the sofa, stood above Hildi. 'You think you are my mother and can speak to me like her, but you can't.' She looked at her glass. 'I need a proper drink, a glass of wine.'

'Don't tell me what to do in my house,' Hildi said, screwing out the cigarette.

'What is it you want?'

'After my loyalty over the years, I was left nothing from your mother. She left me – a glass vase. Can you imagine, that's all she left me.' The pulse in her temple throbbed. 'When she was old, I helped her. When Ted was on top, I arranged for him to draw up her will. All right for me to have a glass vase, but now she owes me something for Ted.'

Hildi went over to the sideboard, threw open the far door. 'You say you want to know about Cousin Ted's recent history. He did the right thing, did what she said. Aimed high, the highest. Had riches.'

She reached for a bulging file; yellowing newspapers and clippings were half falling out as she put it on the sofa, 'Here. Or do you want me to read it? *Corruption on Wall Street. Thousands lose money. Millions of dollars siphoned by broker, Harrison Grey, the junk bond king.* She waved a copy of *The New York Times. Top lawyers accused in biggest crackdown on insider trading*, and Ted's name leads the rest. See, I know all the words by heart.'

Carole put her hands over her face, whispered, 'I didn't know.'

'You know nothing. Ted lost his licence. Lives in Singapore. His wife and children are in New York. I send them money, but the well's run dry. I haven't seen Ted for four years.'

'Terrible. Is there...?'

'Nothing.' A wave of pain cut through Hildi's chest, she bent over. After it ebbed she straightened, ordered the newspapers and, holding them against her breasts, carried the folder back to the sideboard. She waited there, then, 'There's chicken and salad waiting for you in the kitchen. I don't eat.'

'I'm not hungry. I'd like to go to ...'

'You go. Go to bed.' She watched Carole as she climbed the stairs.

From the kitchen came sounds of barking. Yes, the dogs had to go out. Opening the kitchen door she let them into the garden, then went back to the TV room, lit a cigarette. She leaned against the sideboard. 'No jewels. What a terrible loss. Carole is nothing,' she said, letting the smoke dribble out. 'What will Ted do now? Oh God, when will I see him?'

She began to rock. Something was happening. She clamped her mouth shut against it, scrubbed out the cigarette. But she couldn't stop moving. Back and forth – it wouldn't go away. Opening the gate, she doubled over and crawled into the doghouse. A hot smell of dog met her, thick and heavy. Inside her body something was growing, tearing. From the centre of her burst a howl that filled the doghouse.

Tom Downey-eiderdown

Look Right. Left. Right. All clear. Go! Tom shot across the road. He looked back. Yah! He'd done it again! No problem really. Three weeks since he'd started at his new junior school and gone home at noon to have dinner by himself. He'd insisted because school dinners were totally disgusting and his new friend Steve had school dinner alone, so why shouldn't he? His mum had looked worried at first, then said, 'All right, Tom You're nine and know how to cross the street carefully. But, always, always look.' Later, she found a ribbon and hung the house key around his neck. In his heart he liked having dinner at home so he could imagine his father was with him. 'What no jam butties, like when I was child,' he'd hear his dad joke, even though he was now away doing experiments in an American university.

'Ready. Go,' and spreading his arms Tom flew high, then low, jetting around the corner into St Michael's Close. He buzzed past fat Mrs Cousin's house and, holding his satchel, landed next door in front of his newly painted blue front door. Home. But now he had a decision to make – should he eat dinner first, or go see Mrs Joseph about his mum's birthday present? His mum would want him to eat first, but he wouldn't tell her if he didn't. After pulling up his long socks, he ran across the Close, jumped onto Mrs Joseph's kitchen step and knocked. If Mrs Joseph were in, she'd answer.

'Why, Tom, how good to see you.' Mrs Joseph's blue eyes crinkled around the edges.

'Sorry to bother you, Mrs Joseph. I know you're busy preparing your son's dinner, but today is my mum's birthday. I'd like to speak to you for a minute, please.' He opened his satchel and took out two sheets of paper.

'Of course I have time. Ernst comes in fifteen minutes, so do come in.'

Tom followed her into the kitchen with its sweet paprika and onion smell that his nose loved. He'd first smelled it at another visit, and now stood sniffing it again as three long reddish sausages sizzled in the frying pan and white potatoes bubbled fiercely in a pot. How did these sausages taste, he wondered, feeling a rush of spit fill his mouth.

He swallowed, then said, 'I have two recipes. They're my favourites. I'm selling them. I want to buy my mum a present today, before she comes back from her teacher's training,' and he held the papers out to Mrs Joseph.

She wiped her hands on her apron, took the papers. One was underlined in red, Spaghetti Bolognese, and the other in blue, Victoria Sponge. 'Have you copied out your mother's recipes?' she said and her funny 'r' gargled back in her throat. Tom nodded. 'Well, they certainly look as if they will be very good. How much are they?'

'Sixpence each. Mrs Cousins, next door, bought both,' he said.

'Yes. One Italian recipe, one English, and I usually cook German style. Now I shall be International! Come with me to find my purse.' She turned down the gas and ducked under the doorframe to go into the sitting-room. He knew she had to do that because Mrs Joseph was almost as tall and thin as the street lamp in the Close, just the opposite to Mrs Cousins.

The sitting-room was always difficult to get into because of the crowded furniture: a table, two chairs, a sofa, a piano and in the bay window two plumped-up chairs and an old black wooden cabinet covered with little carved flying angels. At his home there was a long sofa, a small table, a record player, a big chair where he read *Swallows and Amazons*. Here books and plants seemed to be growing higgledy-piggledy everywhere, along with lots of small white envelopes that had fallen like snowflakes onto the piano. He followed Mrs Joseph to the wide bay window that looked onto her small garden with its rose bush and blue and pink flowers. While searching for her purse, her head kept nodding up and down like the horse that once came around the Close for rags and bones.

'I forgot where I left my money,' she explained, looking behind a purple plant, and a white one standing on the window-ledge. 'Ah, here's my purse, hidden behind the hyacinth. I was watering it earlier,' and Mrs Joseph gave Tom a shilling. 'Now come for a quick orange drink.'

'You'll like the recipes, I know. I have them for tea often,' and he tucked the shilling in his pocket, next to Mrs Cousin's.

In the kitchen, Mrs Joseph poured out the drink. 'Ernst will come with his litter cart and brush in a few minutes. He leaves them outside the kitchen door. Biscuit?'

'No, thank you. My mum's left me some dinner at home.'

He wanted to ask Mrs Joseph a question about Ernst and his one eye, but decided he would wait for another time.

'Do you like living in St Michael's Close, Tom? Are you happy you moved?'

'My mum and I like it very much. It's so much nicer having a house than a flat, where I had to be quiet and there was no garden. But my father doesn't really know; he's been away for more than two weeks at an American university. He does research, but he'll be back home next week. I wish he didn't go away, but he has to,' and Tom put down the empty glass. 'I hope you don't mind my asking, Mrs Joseph, but why does Ernst always call me, "Tom Downey-eiderdown", when my name is Tom Downey?'

'It is funny, but that is how the Ern knows your name. That's how he remembers it.'

Tom frowned, 'I don't understand. Is that why he speaks funny, like a Dalek?'

'Yes, that is part of his story.'

From outside came the sound of wheels scraping against the pavement. Ernst had come and Tom realised he'd stayed too long.

Today going to school, he'd seen Ernst bouncing up and down pushing the Council's litter cart, shovelling in sweetie papers, empty bottles, dog poo. Ernst had said 'hello' to him and, as always, had thick sweat running down his face. And Wayne Price, the school bully, was standing there laughing at him. 'I bet he's your best friend,' he said. But Ernst wasn't his friend.

'I'll go home now, Mrs Joseph,' Tom said. But there was no time to escape as Ernst had pushed open the door, filling the room.

'Hello, Mutti,' he shouted in his Dalek voice, then, 'Hello, Tom Downey-eiderdown. Today, October 2nd 1968, is your mother's birthday. Your telephone number is 954 2725.'

Ernst's live brown eye looked into his, while the other one was like the bottom of a milk bottle. Tom couldn't bear the dead eye and looked away.

'My Ernst, go upstairs and wash, change your shirt. Dinner is ready.'

'First I have a present.' He bounced into the sitting-room, looked around at the scattered white envelopes. When he came to the top of the piano, he looked closely and pointed enthusiastically to an envelope, 'Mrs Downey-eiderdown.' Then he turned and rushed up the stairs.

Mrs Joseph smiled, 'Tom, everyone in the Close receives a small chocolate bar for a birthday present. For the Ern, it is very important. Please take the envelope and give it to your mother.'

He took it, but before squeezing it into his pocket saw that the large letters were shaped like his own writing. 'I have to go now, Mrs Joseph. Thank you.'

'Please come again.'

Sitting in his kitchen, Tom popped a handful of crisps in his mouth, drank some milk. He combined the carrots and boiled potatoes and smashed them into the fish fingers to disguise the taste. I bet Mrs Joseph's sausages taste better than this rubbish, he thought. His father made a funny face when he saw him smash his food, while his mum was always telling him to hurry up and finish.

Mrs Joseph didn't seem ever to hurry, but then she was old, more than fifty probably. He would ask his mother, when she returned from college, why some people were always nervous and others calm. His mum wasn't quiet either, maybe because his father was away from home so much. With a thrust of his fork Tom shovelled in another mouthful and chewed. But Mrs Joseph didn't seem to have a husband. In his month in the Close, he'd never seen him. Was he new to England, too? He and his mum and dad were new to the Close, but not to England, and with a gulp the mouthful went down. Mr Joseph was probably very old, probably dead. He was lucky his father wasn't dead. Today, for his mum's birthday, there'd be a telephone call from him. A really special day and he pushed the plate away.

Putting his hand in his pocket, he jiggled the two shillings. Enough money for his mum's favourite sweets, *After Eight Mints*. After school he'd bicycle down to the shop at the bottom of the road and buy them. She should be home by then, and that gave him a warm feeling inside. He looked at his plate and scraped the rest into the rubbish bin. An apple was waiting for him. In Break he'd eat it and kick a football with his friend Steve. Holding his satchel, Tom closed the door. He waited at the curb. Look Right. Left. Right. All Clear!

The box of *After Eight Mints* bounced inside his grey shirt as Tom bicycled towards his house. He waved as he passed Mrs Joseph pushing her wicker shopping basket. Seeing their Ford

Popular parked outside meant his mum was home, so leaving the bike in the garage he ran to the open front door, tiptoed inside. The card was in his satchel and he put it together with the parcel and shouted, 'Mum.'

'Hello, darling,' and she ran downstairs, hair flying. 'I didn't know you were back.'

'Happy Birthday,' and he held out the present.

She took it, her eyes open wide and, holding the paper bag carefully, lifted the green box. '*After Eights*, my favourites,' she cried. Then Tom took the card with its circling, whirling designs in orange, blue and green and read aloud, 'To Mum, A Very Happy Birthday. Love and kisses from, Tom.'

His mother's arms were around him and she held him so tight until all his breath was gone. 'Thank you, darling. Thank you so much. What a lovely surprise! Can we have one now? I'll make a cup of tea, you have some juice and we'll have an *After Eight* for tea.'

He felt swollen with happiness.

'I'm sorry I keep forgetting to give you your pocket money. How did you have so much money?' His mum was looking at him, her eyes all happy.

He told her about selling her best recipes to Mrs Cousins and Mrs Joseph.

'How nice that they bought them,' she smiled.

'I told them they were my favourites. There's a chocolate from Ernst too,' and he fished it out of his pocket.

She looked at the squashed penny cream bar. 'How kind of him,' and her face went pink as she put it down to pour the tea.

'He gives a sweetie to everyone on their birthday. Calls you Mrs Downey-eiderdown.'

'I know, Mrs Joseph told me. Ernst was very ill, years ago. Had a very serious operation; that is why he has only one eye. He should have been brilliant. But he's happy, loves his work cleaning streets. Mrs Joseph is a very strong woman.'

'Not as strong as Ernst. He shouted, made a big fist when Wayne Price threw an apple core at him. Wayne just escaped.'

'Wayne shouldn't have done that. Now, here's your juice.' Then she opened the box. 'For you, Tom,' and she gave him a brown paper with a thin chocolate mint.

He took it out, held the square for a second, let it fall into his mouth. Eyes and mouth closed – it melted into a pool of sweetness, the bitter chocolate and the mint flowing together over his tongue and down his throat. What a great idea buying it. After the mint was gone, he opened his eyes, licked his fingers. His mum was grinning at him with chocolate brown teeth and he laughed so hard he fell onto the floor.

The phone was ringing. His mum shouted, 'It might be David!' Tom scrambled to his feet and ran with her to the lounge. Phone in hand, she sank in the sofa, while he couldn't stop moving about the room. Looking out of the window, he watched the sky, the white clouds rushing away from him. How long did the clouds take until they reached America? His mother's laughter was flying off into the air, too.

'Thank you, darling, I'm having a lovely birthday. A delicious chocolate present from Tom. How is the work going?...Another three weeks? I thought you'd be home next ... Yes, of course, there are scientific reasons. Please write a long letter explaining them or I shall wonder, and worry. We're well but lonely. I love you too. Here's Tom.'

His father's gravelly voice asked questions, as usual.

'I'm okay ... School? Our football team is worthless. In our last game we lost four nil. Wayne Price was goalie. A disaster. For her birthday, I gave Mum *After Eights*. I had one just now. It was great, but they'll all be gone if you don't come home soon ... It's boring without you ... I'm trying ... Me too. Bye.'

Tom looked at his mum; her eyes were dark brown. She reached over to him, her fingers moved slowly down his cheek.

'When will he really come home?'

'Soon.'

His throat hurt. Why couldn't his father sell shoes in North Harrow like Steve's dad?

The next day Tom ate his chicken breast and carrot dinner quickly; the empty house felt cold after yesterday's excitement. He went for a spin around the Close, and there was Mrs Joseph coming around the corner pushing her shopping basket.

'Hello, Mrs Joseph,' he called. 'Yesterday, we spoke to my father. All the way to America. My mum liked my present,' and he rode over to meet her. 'I'll help you, if you like,' and got off his bike.

'It's not heavy,' she said, biting the words while unlocking the kitchen door.

'I'm strong for my age, but not like Ernst.'

'That'll do. Not today.' It was a snapping 'No' voice.

He jumped off the kitchen step, ran to his bicycle.

Her quiet voice called out from behind, 'Tom, I'm sorry. Would you like an orange drink?'

He nodded.

'Please come in. I need a cup of coffee.' Then he saw Mrs Joseph's face was the colour of sick.

He slowly walked into the house. The water was in the pot on the cooker.

A metal grinder was attached to the wall, and Mrs Joseph turned the handle, grinding beans. 'I received some unpleasant news this morning, so I too became unpleasant. That's foolish, isn't it?' Her face was still a bad colour when she turned to him. 'I'm sorry, Tom. Here you are,' and she poured out the orange and water, then took a jug, put the coffee in a paper filter, adding the boiling water.

He followed her into the lounge, sliding past the sofa and piano.

'Do sit down. Have some biscuits.'

The chair sank under him and he reached for a half-moon biscuit. He couldn't find any words so he took a bite, a drink, and watched Mrs Joseph drinking her coffee.

'I was angry because today there was a letter from the Council telling Ernst that he is not to work cleaning the streets any longer. Tomorrow is his last day. They're afraid that he isn't careful enough and will be run over.'

'But he cleans the streets very well. He likes collecting the rubbish, making it into neat piles.'

'I explained that to them, but the Council has made up its mind.'

'What will Ernst do?'

'I'll tell him tonight.'

Tom saw her long, thin neck. He wanted to tell her not to say anything, that Ernst could get very angry. But she interrupted him by holding out a chocolate biscuit in the shape of a star, and he took it.

'These are called Lebkuchen – spice cookies from Germany.'

'Ernst's strong, he might use …'

'I know the Ernst.' She carefully put down her cup, leaned back in the chair, closed her shining eyes.

Tom watched her. What did she mean? Of course she knew him – he's big and fat and he might go mad because it wasn't fair. That's what children do, get angry, hit you. He felt himself getting all itchy. In front of him was the black wooden sideboard and on it were carved flying angels. Boys don't fly like angels, didn't she know that?

Mrs Joseph sat up and finished her coffee. 'Tom, I'm afraid it's time to go back to school. Thank you very much for keeping me company when I needed it.'

'It wasn't fair what they did about Ernst.' He opened the door, jumped off the kitchen steps and picked up his bike. He'd tell his mum about what happened.

School football practice had been horrible. He'd been made goalie for yelling at thick Wayne Price, who'd missed stopping three goals straight in a row. Then he, too, allowed two goals in. He was so angry at himself he wanted to shout, even ran home without looking carefully. To top it, today his mum was home early and very busy doing her stupid teaching practice preparation. He took his milk and sandwich up to his room and slammed the door.

Each bit of his rotten kit he threw into the corner. 'Football stinks,' he shouted, kicking the pile of rubbish. Afterwards he sat down at his desk, looked down onto the Close. It wasn't right. His father wasn't here. Instead he was always away working on his stupid experiments. Tom glued his eyes on the cars going down the road, mostly ugly old Fords and Vauxhalls. Boring tea would be ready soon. There was a rattling sound, wheels that scraped, and around the corner he saw Ernst pushing his cart, the big brush standing straight like a flag. He'd forgotten him, and tonight Ernst was going home to hear he'd lost his job. Tomorrow will be his last day.

Tom watched him go bouncing along towards Mrs Joseph's kitchen. The light was on, probably she was making his supper with delicious red sausages. He saw him open the door, heard, 'Mutti!' Now what would happen? Goose bumps raced up and down his back.

He ran into his parents' room. His mum was busy writing, surrounded by grey and blue notebooks. 'Help, Mummy. Help!'

She got up. 'Tom, what's the matter?'

'Ernst is going to hurt Mrs Joseph. I know it. The Council won't let him clean the streets anymore. He'll hit her when she tells him. We should call the police.'

She took his hand and they sat down on the bed. 'That's terrible. I'm so sorry about his job, but Ernst may not become angry. Tom, don't you think we'd better wait and see what happens? Ernst is strong, but Mrs Joseph understands him. She'll know what to do. We can always call for help, if necessary, but Mrs Joseph wouldn't want that now. It'll be all right, dear. Let's wait a little.'

Tom bit his lip. His mother was full of books, she didn't understand.

'We'll need our strength, so let's have tea,' and she got up. 'Please set the table. The potatoes have boiled. I'll put up the chipolatas and peas.'

Setting out the forks and knives, everything was as always, so he went out into the front garden to see if the Close was quiet. A few early lights were on, just the same. Still, it was too bad his father wasn't here right now ... Of course he'd come back soon. He said he would ... Above him, the October orange sky was light and he went back inside, leaving the door open to let in the clean air.

He finished a mouthful of chipolatas. 'Mum, Mrs Joseph has red sausages with spices in them, they smell great, can we try them once?'

'If Budgen's carries them, I'll buy them. Sorry, Tom, but I haven't time to go to a special shop for them. Tonight I'm behind with my preparation. Let's finish quickly so we can all go back to our homework. Try not to worry about Ernst, put it away for now, all right?'

A shout. The peas fell off Tom's fork. Across the Close

Mrs Joseph's voice was speaking, clear and firm, in what Tom thought was German. She was answering Ernst, speaking to his shouting anger. Silence. Then a loud cry and Mrs Joseph was calling, 'Halte! Nein, Ernst. Nein.' Tom heard her voice crack, then go quiet. He looked at his mum, she was pale but stayed still. His fingers kept pulling at each other.

He somehow knew what Mrs Joseph was saying – it was about Ernst's pain, that she understood him, that screaming wouldn't help, there were other answers. Again her words came clearly as Ernst yelled. Her words standing against the wail of his cries. Then Ernst began to be quiet, cried out again, became silent. Mrs Joseph kept on speaking firmly in her distant German words.

Tom pushed his plate away, put his arms on the table and laid his head on them. He heard his mother's chair scrape back, felt her soft body touching his as she ran her hand down his back, her lips on his hair.

'I'll clear the things now,' she said quietly. But he could hear her clashing the plates – dropping forks, knives, in the kitchen.

Tom wondered how all that feeling would end. Was the anger going on, with white birthday envelopes being torn, chocolate pieces flying in the air? Or were Ernst and Mrs Joseph tied together in blood? He got up. His head felt too heavy for his neck, it wobbled as he went upstairs to his room. In the dark he dropped his clothes on the floor, crawled into bed. After what seemed forever, his mum came in to kiss him goodnight. But voices still came into his head, some crying.

TOM DOWNEY-EIDERDOWN

On his way to school in the morning Tom saw that the people in the Close seemed to be walking with an effort. At Mrs Joseph's house the milk bottle was still outside. Today his mother decided to be late for college and crossed the road with him, walking him to school.

At dinnertime he carefully crossed the road, but sitting in front of his favourite tuna, lettuce, mayonnaise sandwich, he wasn't hungry. He ran out of the house and across the Close.

The milk bottle was still there, and Mrs Joseph's kitchen door was closed. Tom knocked, waited, his heart banging.

'Mrs Joseph, it's me,' he called. 'Sorry to disturb you. I just wanted to know how you are?'

The door opened a little, Mrs Joseph leaned against it. 'I'm all right, Tom. That's very nice of you to ask.'

She was smiling, but on her cheek was a large blue and red bruise and wrapped around her neck was a scarf, a bandage sticking out from under it.

'Ernst hit you.'

'It's nothing. We were noisy, but now the Ernst understands why this happened and that we must go on. That is the main thing.' The wind was blowing bits of her brown-grey hair across her face. 'He is interested in numbers, we will find challenging things for him. He will do well.'

'I'm sorry to bother you, but I was worried.'

'Thank you. Today I won't invite you in, the house is upside down. But come any other time. Now I must look at the potatoes. Ernst will soon be back from work and I want his dinner to be ready.'

Tom jumped off the steps, ran back across the Close. He felt much better; he'd seen Mrs Joseph. She wasn't dead. He was about to go inside when he thought – things will be different for Mrs Joseph, but still she wasn't angry with Ernst. She didn't hold it against him, even when he'd hurt her face and neck. She was just the same, making dinner for him as usual. Wasn't that funny?

From around the corner came a familiar scraping sound, Ernst coming with his rubbish cart and brush for the last time. Tom's legs wanted to run. He didn't want to look at the sweaty face, the big hands, the dead eye. He listened to the squeaking wheels.

'Hello, Ernst.'

'Hello, Tom Downey-eiderdown. 954.2725.'

The Death Hat

Sara Lovejoy smoothed down the bedspread ready for her first summer paying guest. When Mrs Thomas, who taught grade school, waved goodbye to go on summer vacation, she left the room empty until September. After the curtains were washed and the room given an extra sweep, it occurred to Mrs Lovejoy that a few summer visitors might like to come and stay at her New Hampshire farm. So she put an advertisement in 'The Lake Winnipesaukee and District Bulletin for Visitors', offering a pleasant, quiet room here in New Shrewsbury at Silver Farm.

Only yesterday a Mr Miner telephoned. A hard voice, with a kind of twang in it, mentioned that he'd read her notice and would like to come to stay for a week, or even longer if it suited him. Yes indeed, she answered, and offered to welcome him this morning at the New Shrewsbury bus stop at seven twenty-five or later in the day at four twenty-five. He'd chosen the afternoon. He must be an older man, she decided, to be in a position to afford the twenty dollars a week for room and board. But when she told Mr Lovejoy about him, he'd started shouting, 'No more strangers. I've had enough strangers.' So she'd informed him quite plainly that cash in hand in 1954 was very important, especially because of his illness. She was the one who'd be doing the extra washing and cooking, not him, so he'd better swallow his anger and be still. He turned his wheelchair around and rode out of the room.

From downstairs came the noise of the final spin from the milk separator. As Mrs Lovejoy came into the kitchen the machine juddered to a stop, splashing the last of today's cream on to the sides of the glass container. She poured the yellow foam into a large jug ready for the blueberry pie tonight. The separating was already finished; soon time for Betty to take the heavy milk cans outside for collection.

The jug went in the fridge, the empty glass in the sink, and she lit the oven under the pan of beans. Money was hard to come by, especially since they'd cut down on the number of milkers they kept. Her daughter had to look after them alone now, on account of Mr Lovejoy's stroke. But Betty was a big girl and able to do a man-size job, although the day was barely long enough for her to take care of a herd of cows, give a hand in the vegetable garden when needed and keep the accounts. The guest's money would help, with luck there'd be others and that gave Mrs Lovejoy a positive feeling which hadn't been there for a while. The kitchen clock said four-twenty, nearly time for Mr Miner's arrival on the Franklin to Concord bus. In the mirror she gave her hair a quick pat and set off to wait in the late afternoon sunshine.

The old bus let out a black puff of exhaust smoke as it braked at the stop and one small, thin man got off. Her sight wasn't good, but she could make out that the man's hair was a light yellow, not at all grey. He was wearing brown pants with a khaki-coloured jacket and he must have seen her because he stood still for a moment, seeming to wait for her to do something. Walking always made the sciatica in her left leg needle up, and to ease it she took just a step towards him. Now he walked swiftly towards her, holding a brown suitcase. It was clear that he was young, yes, really very young. As he came close, she caught a quick breath. Looking past his bright blue eyes, the skin around his nose and cheeks was hatched with deep scars.

'Arlo Miner, coming for a room, Ma'am,' he said smiling, and held out his hand. She took it, saw that two of his teeth were missing.

His mom should tell him to see a dentist, she thought. Pumping his hand she said, 'I'm Sara Lovejoy, this is Silver Farm,' and pointed to the white shingled house. 'Now, come on along. My husband's there waiting and daughter Betty is finishing the chores. Just time to get settled. Supper is always at six,' and she opened the door into the hall. 'Did you have a good bus ride?'

'Could be worse.'

Upstairs in the guestroom, the blue and white curtains puffed in and out in the warm breeze. At the foot of the double bed lay the old family patchwork quilt.

'Here we are,' she welcomed.

As he put down his suitcase, whatever was inside gave a resounding clink. Looking at his face, she decided it would be polite to ignore the sound. Instead she explained, 'Across the hall are the toilet and bath, all shared. Our bedroom's next door, if you need anything, just knock. There's your towel. Our farm sells dairy products. Behind the barn there's a wood – it's pine and birch mostly with a pond for small fishing and swimming. You can walk there, but take care of the cows in the field, they're not always friendly.' But she saw the young man wasn't really listening, rather was looking at the stern face in the framed picture hanging over the bed.

'A relative?'

'Oh, no, no,' she laughed. 'That's Daniel Webster, a famous man from these parts, way back. Spoke of liberty and the union of the United States, one and inseparable. Well, you'll want to unpack now. Use the chest of drawers. There's a bell rung for dinner at six. Are there any questions, Mr Miner?'

'Is there a key to the room, Ma'am,' he blurted.

Her mouth twitched a smile, both at his way of talking through his nose and his request. Really, just a boy. In all the years she'd rented to teachers, they never once asked for a key. 'I have a drawer full of odd keys, I'll have a look.'

'Thank you and please call me Arlo. Do you want the twenty dollars now, or at the end of the week?' From his pocket he took out a wallet swollen with bills.

She'd never seen so much money, was torn needing it and feeling her face go red asking. Thanking him, she gently slid the bill into her apron pocket. 'I'll give you a receipt at supper. I hope you don't mind my saying, Arlo, but you speak different than we do.'

'Yes, Ma'am. I was born in Missouri.'

'Of course, that accounts for it. New Hampshire is a long way …'

'Yes.'

'I hope you like it here.'

'I reckon I will.'

He closed the door behind her.

At dinner it was warm in the kitchen, and Mrs Lovejoy set out a platter of eggs and bacon with the baked beans. She'd spoken to the family about the guest's scarred face, so Betty in her friendly way broke through the silence. She filled in about the farm – how much milk the cows gave daily, the number of eggs the hens laid, also her concern that winter feed would be going up. Of course, when Betty finished they heard the clock ticking. The young man wasn't a great talker, hadn't seen much of life yet, she expected, but he did once make an effort.

He was looking into his empty plate, 'I must've eaten a ton of canned beans in the past four years, but I judge this is the first time I've had home-made baked beans.'

'Baked beans and New England just go together. You'll see, we eat them a lot,' and they laughed, except for Mr Lovejoy, who sat in his wheelchair with his lips tightly shut.

'Pops, your favourite dessert is waiting – blueberry pie.' Betty took off her glasses, polished them, all the while smiling.

'Food don't interest me any more. All I am is stuck here without anyone bothering about me.' In front of him, Mr Lovejoy was watching the white of his egg swim in the broken yolk.

'All right, you just leave it,' said Mrs Lovejoy. 'Now, if we're all finished, Betty can clear. The pie and cream are ready and waiting,' and she picked up a knife to cut a large triangle. The blue juice spilled out of the pie as the slice went on the plate. 'Here you are, Arlo. The berries grow wild here. You can pick some, if you want.'

'Blueberries don't grow in Crève-Coeur Park in St. Louis,' he said, pouring on the cream, making the pie become a floating island.

'Hear that? Now, Betty, your turn.' Already half the pie was gone and Mrs Lovejoy filled a dessert spoon full of berries and cream, and gave it to her husband. The berries oozed from his lips, the juice sliding through the stubble onto his chin. Taking away the spoon, she took her napkin and mopped it up. 'Hope you're not shocked, Mr Miner. It's not easy for Mr Lovejoy, after his stroke four months ago.'

'Never shocked, Ma'am.'

That's nice, she thought. He's not snickering, like many young men would.

'Pops, after supper the radio.' Betty leaned over towards Arlo, putting her milker's hands on the table. 'We haven't got television yet, but at night we listen to the farming news, sometimes the world. If you're interested you can join …'

'That's really kind. But it's still light outside, just right for a walk. Look around. I'd like that.'

Mrs Lovely smoothed down her hair. 'Of course you must do what you want, it's your vacation. Along the road is always nice, the birds still singing. Only a few cars. I'm sorry there isn't a place with one of those old jukeboxes, but this state's dry except for package stores.'

'Forewarned is forearmed.' Arlo laughed a single laugh.

'The pie was very good, Ma'am. Now if you'll excuse me,' and after folding his napkin, he got up.

'Please, when you go out or come in, use the kitchen door, it's always unlocked. And here's your receipt. I also found a key for your room – so many, all higgledy piggledy.' Mrs Lovejoy reached across with the slip of paper and a large key. 'Remember this is country. No lights at night, just stars.'

'I know. Summer – not too hot, and no one here to shoot at me.'

'Good heavens! Of course not.'

'Thank you for supper.'

Mrs Lovejoy watched him go out into the pink sky evening. 'What a peculiar thing to say.' Then she pushed herself out of the chair, collected the dessert plates, and turned on the faucet.

'Seems a nice young man, don't you think?' said Betty.

'Better than some, I'd say. Needs looking after. We'll feed him up this week. But I'm worried there won't be much for him to do.'

Mr Lovejoy muttered, 'I've not seen cold burns like that for years. Last time was when Billy Hicks got lost two days in a freak ice storm up Mount Washington, nearly froze to death. Face got blistered, then broke, got infected. Too bad for a young man to look like that, to come here and not want excitement.'

'You never said that about excitement and me, Pops.'

'You're a woman. And the Second World War was on when you were his age. 1954 is different – singers like Elvis Presley, the kids screaming, that's what the young do.'

'Maybe the young man doesn't want excitement,' and Mrs Lovejoy handed Betty the plates.

'Until today, I never met a young man who isn't push ahead, and full of himself,' she said.

'Why has he come here?' asked Mrs Lovejoy.

Mr Lovejoy snorted, 'To see new parts … Get away from a big city. Do you know anything about St. Louis, Bet?'

'It's a port city. Lots of Germans came to make beer and shoes. Before them were the French. The city was named after their king, I think.'

'The Mississippi River?'

'Yes. I always wanted to see it. Maybe I should go out there myself, to see new parts. What do you think, Pops?' She was smiling.

'Don't talk rubbish. Who'd look after the farm, now as I can't?'

'Arlo has money of his own, I saw it. Lots of it,' explained Mrs Lovejoy.

'I could have money too, if I had a paying job …'

'Betty!'

'Just joking, Mom. Maybe he stole it.'

'He doesn't act like a thief, too polite,' and Mrs Lovejoy hung up the towel. 'Dishes over. Thinking about Arlo kept us going, didn't it?'

'We missed the farming news.'

'Tomorrow, Mr Lovejoy. Now come on upstairs, time for bed. Betty, before you go and see to the cows, give us a hand. I'm tired out.'

But lying beside her husband, Mrs Lovejoy couldn't sleep. Catnaps mostly in the first part of the night, then later between his snores she was kept awake by odd sounds. Not anything very noisy from next door, but rather loud whisperings, a voice talking. Probably Arlo being lonely, talking to himself. Then, drifting off, she caught not only very bad words spoken, but also what resembled animal cries, and she woke up again. She mustn't make the bed creak too much for Mr Lovejoy could wake up in spite of the pills, and that would mean an endless night. So she lay straight and heavy in the darkness listening, waiting until the last of the whimpering next door quieted.

In the day Arlo was an easy guest, leaving after breakfast and taking a couple of sandwiches for lunch. Betty said he told her that he enjoyed going into the woods to pass the day. Then, late in the afternoon Mrs Lovejoy saw him picking his way across the field, his hair wet from swimming, returning in time for supper. With the family he usually sat almost wordless, although Betty did her best to encourage him.

'Have any brothers and sisters, Arlo?' she said, leaning forward.

A hesitation, then, 'Four brothers, five sisters. Haven't seen them for a while.'

'That's really big,' Mr Lovejoy said. 'Must be something good in that Mississippi water.' He laughed and laughed.

'Oh, Pops.'

'Don't be a killjoy, Betty. First good laugh I've had in a long while,' he shouted.

Mrs Lovejoy had to smile, then looking at Arlo's face, she stopped.

Late at night in his locked room was when Mrs Lovejoy heard him speak, and in loud whispers croak ugly swear words to someone or other. They were terrible words, so full of bile and hate that she tried to cover her ears not to hear. Once he must have moved his bed, hit the wall and cried out, promising he'd kill someone.

Tonight, as she pulled her nightgown around her she was frightened by his cries again. Mr Lovejoy might waken, have another stroke. And after four nights listening to choked screams and hoarse shouts, she decided she had to do something. Waiting until there was a long silence, she pushed out of bed, went across to her daughter's room and opened the door.

At once Betty woke up. 'Pops? Something wrong?'

'No, no, he's all right, asleep. It's Arlo. At night, are you kept awake by him?'

'I don't hear him. My room's too far away. He goes to the john a lot, though.'

'He says terrible things. About killing people. I don't know if I can put up with it for three more nights. I'm afraid how he got all that money.'

'Mom, he's young, maybe lonely. I'm sure he's not bad. Have a word with him.' She reached over to touch the rough skin on her mother's arm.

'In the day, he is always very nice and polite. But I can't sleep. Tomorrow I'll go and see what he's got in his room, just in case …'

'You can't do that, he's paid for it. You gave him the key.'

Mrs Lovejoy bent down, 'Found the old door keys are all the same, fit all the locks. Tomorrow, when you go to the barn, push your father up there. I don't want him in the house when I look.'

After lunch everyone was away, but when fitting in the key her fingers fumbled. As the door was opened, it gave a squeak she'd never noticed before. There standing in front of her, like a bowling pin, was an empty bottle of Southern Comfort. She stepped in and that sent a second bottle bouncing, followed by a third, both smacking against the far wall. But the bottles missed the row of dollar bills that had been put there. She couldn't believe it, but different stacks of money were set out along the skirting board, all ordered, lined up in a neat row. Going closer she saw one hundred dollar bills, then fifties, then twenties, tens, fives, all set in neat piles. But everything else in the room had been turned upside down.

To stop crying out, she thrust her hands over her mouth. The chair had been turned over, the table upside down, great Daniel Webster's picture was face down on the floor along with the sheets and the precious quilt. The bed had been moved, leaving a small space behind it. In God's name what did it all mean? Fear gripped her. There was the brown suitcase. She must pull herself together, look inside.

Gently, she lifted the lid of the case, her heart knocking at the wrong she was doing. But she must find out, remember to put everything back as she found it. God only knew what he'd do otherwise. Careful, careful, and she took out his pants, put them onto the floor and discovered two more Southern Comforts wrapped in a shirt and sweater. She lifted out the bottles. More clothes went on the floor. At the bottom, the last thing there was what looked like a hat, the strangest hat she'd ever seen. It was almost peaked – sheepskin most likely with its white fur flaps for covering the ears, long strings to tie it on. She picked it up, one flap hung by a thread. As she turned the hat around, her throat froze. Bullet holes were through the front. Inside the hat the wool was stiff with blood – and from it rose a dead fish smell. She rushed to the window to breathe. Dear God, Arlo had killed the man wearing the hat. And there he was walking across the field in the direction of the kitchen. She dropped the hat, ran.

Holding tightly to the banister she moved quickly downstairs. 'I must make him go now,' she said. But the clock was striking quarter to six. The law of supper, they'd be waiting for it no matter what. She made herself go into the kitchen, but she had trouble cutting the ham, in front of her the black holes in the hat. Then she remembered the open suitcase. What would Arlo do? She tried to pull herself together, focus her mind.

'Hi there, Ma'am. Enjoyed your sandwiches. Nothing cleaner than a swim. Be down in a few minutes for dinner,' and, waving, he was gone before she could stop him. The open suitcase! She had to tell Betty. Automatically she lit the oven, shoved in the beans and hurried to the barn.

At supper they sat in quiet at the table. Mrs Lovejoy, picking at her napkin, knew she had to begin. 'Arlo, I heard from Mrs Thomas, the schoolteacher who always stays here. She's coming back from her vacation tomorrow,' she said. 'I'm sorry, but I'll need her room back. Would you please leave then. Of course, I'll return the money.'

Arlo looked at his hands, flexed them.

'I'm sorry to ask you ... She's lived here for years.' Mrs Lovejoy looked up. Around her, silence. Arlo was chewing the insides of his cheeks. She watched him, fear crawling down her back.

'I locked my door. You opened it.'

She sank down in her chair. Then with all her energy, she made herself sit up. 'Yes, I did. I had to. Things were wrong. At night there were too many loud and disturbing cries coming from your room. Threats, hate. I couldn't sleep.'

'I can't ever sleep.' He wasn't apologising.

'With the terrible thing you've done, I couldn't sleep either.' The accusing words gave her courage.

'Oh, no, no.' Making a hard fist, he began drumming on the table. 'With bugles screeching, they came at us like ants. Thousands screaming. Never stopping. Fucking yellow mongrels!'

'Who?'

'The mother-fucking Chinese soldiers ...'

Mrs Lovejoy frowned, 'What are you talking about?'

He stared at her. 'It's you who know nothing. Have you forgotten the war?'

She looked at her husband.

Arlo shouted, 'Korea. You fucking dumbbell. The Korean

War. Just a year ago. And you've fucking forgot Chosin, Heartbreak Ridge. Fifty thousand Americans dead. You ignorant bitch.'

Now he was standing, body shaking. He turned away from the table, trying to control himself, find his breath. 'I'm twenty-two. Four years in the infantry. My platoon nine months behind the enemy's line, so far north each breath hurt.' He turned to Mr Lovejoy, crying, 'For Christ's sake you should understand … In battles the bastards came and came … so many bodies, so many Americans. Chinese. So cold my cheeks froze off. Let me die. Let me die. Christ, all bad things. I want to forget the bad things, but I can't.' He ran out of the kitchen door.

Mrs Lovejoy looked at Betty, Mr Lovejoy. They sat. But Betty had to see to the cows. Mr Lovejoy had to go to bed. Mrs Lovejoy got up.

Lying in bed the hours crawled by waiting for steps on the stairs, for the usual noises to come from his room. When the early sun was shining under the bedroom curtain, Mrs Lovejoy heard him return. Moving as quietly as possible, she got out of bed and put on her cotton wrap.

The door was open. His back was to her. The room had been set in order. He was bending over the suitcase putting in a shirt.

She wet her lips, swallowed. 'Arlo, I'm sorry. I didn't know you were in Korea defending our country.'

He didn't turn, kept on putting in pants, bottles. 'It's okay, Mrs Lovejoy. In life we all know different things … you cows, dairies … me …'

'I'm sorry. Somehow I've even forgotten where Korea is ... It's so far away from here.'

'Okay.'

Taking a step towards him, she offered the twenty-dollar bill. 'Here. Change your mind and stay.'

He straightened, and when he turned the sheepskin hat was in his hand. Seeing the black crusted inside, she shut her eyes.

'Thanks, M'am, I won't stay. I'll get the early bus.' Then he went over to the far wall with its ordered money. 'Mine,' and he pressed the hundreds, fifty, twenty, ten, five-dollar bills, deep inside the hat. When he finished, he nodded. 'My death hat,' and carefully placed it in his suitcase. 'While I still have some of my pay, I'll keep on travelling. Otherwise I'd feel obliged to share with my family. The blood money belongs to me. You see how I deserve it.' He bent down and closed the suitcase. 'Please say goodbye to your family.'

Holding the handle of the brown suitcase, he went down the stairs. From the window she watched the suitcase swinging as he headed towards the bus stop.

She felt wrung out, too weak to clean the room. As she closed the door, she looked at her fist. There it was, his twenty-dollar bill. It felt wet, sticky in her hand. No, no, she mustn't keep it. She must return it and went quickly down the stairs. The kitchen clock read twenty-three past seven.

Rushing down the path, needles thrust into her leg. She had to reach him. Across the road the stop sign was empty. As she ran the black smoke from the moving bus caught her in the throat. She stopped to gasp in air. The bus drove on. Again she ran after it. Her legs folding, Mrs Lovejoy held up the bill, 'Arlo, your blood mon...'

The Yellow Brick House

At seventy-one, Julia should be at home in the yellow brick house. She should be lying on the sofa, bought by her father second-hand in 1939 for two guineas and reupholstered twice by her mother. She should be drinking a cup of tea from the last of the family Staffordshire china while resting her hip, and covered by the rug she'd crocheted. Instead, she was trotting around the Benjamin Britten Council Estate doing market research, and that was all wrong, her friend Lola kept telling her. But here she was standing in front of another grey door and professionally announcing, 'Market research', and not receiving any answer.

As instructed, Julia had arrived at two o'clock and since then only one woman had agreed to be interviewed, although several had shouted 'too busy'. Now it was after six and again she wrote 'NA' in the file. But she mustn't complain – ever since retiring from teaching English at the local comprehensive, it was interviewing that paid the mortgage on the yellow brick house. So, hoisting her rucksack onto her back and pulling down her hood, Julia headed into the spitting rain, the oldest hoodie in England.

A bridge to cross, then several flats, and with luck she'd find someone to chat with before asking him/her to fill out the survey on 'Your Bank, its services and you'. So far today, the sole interviewee had been a sweet young woman, originally from Northern Ireland, a pretty mum with a baby called Skye. Yesterday's best was an old man full of laughs and coughs, who told her how he'd once assembled the 'back end' of cars in Luton.

Facing the last flat Julia squinted through the squares of glass and rang. No answer. As if on cue her stomach tightened, followed by a scraping pain in her left hip. Disappointment and the damp always made her arthritis worse. 'Enough!' she announced to no one, 'Let's go home!' Seven interviews done in the last three days and by tomorrow's deadline she'd find the last three. So, time to drive home, and see how her friend Lola was feeling after her gallstone op.

November darkness crowded around her as she edged down the stairs, gripping the metal railing to avoid slipping on fried chicken scraps and squashed coffee cups. She went slowly, her mind counting the money she'd be paid – all of it going towards the mortgage. Now satisfied, the matter of supreme importance became her darling Mike. He'd be arriving at the house early tomorrow morning, have time at home before driving off Monday for his next performance. 'My actor son.' Just saying the words aloud was important, it connected her to the great wide world.

Julia slung her rucksack over her shoulder and headed down the worn flagstone path to the yellow brick house. Forever her home, since her father rented it before he shipped away in the War. Here, she and mother waited for his return, which never came. To live, her mother taught at the local infant school and when Julia was old enough, they began gardening together – potatoes, beans, squash, Jerusalem artichokes. These gifts the soil had always given them. That is what she wanted now – the pleasure of sitting in her kitchen with Lola, eating the magic garden soup she made last night.

On opening the kitchen door, she found no sign of her friend, although everything was ordered and neat. She was about to call when jabbing needles ran through her hip, making her sit down. She rocked back and forth, her hand trying to soothe the pain away. Finally, she was again able to focus and there on the table, along with a bunch of letters, was a note sticking out of a jam jar. *Hi Sweetie, I know you're busy, so I tidied up. I'm really better now, so thanks again for letting me stay. A true friend! It was just like old times when you used to come to my Yoga classes and we had time to talk. I also ate your magic soup – delicious. Now I'm off to bed again and a good sleep. Love to your handsome son. xxx Lola.*

Their thirty years of friendship held many shades of sadness and joy. She pushed herself out of the chair, limped over to the cooker to watch the aquarium of chicken and garden vegetables swim around the pot. Bubbles rose as she dipped in the ladle to fill her bowl.

After a final scraping, she leaned back in the captain's chair, yawned. This would be the perfect moment to curl up for a snooze, but on the table she recognised an envelope from The Central Building Society – the red capitals demanded attention. She unfolded the single sheet. *Due to changing fiscal circumstances, we regret that there will be a change in the standard variable rate on 40 Shaw Road, Horton, Hertfordshire by 0.5%, to 4.75%, starting from the first of January...* Her left eye twitched.

Money. The interest-only payment on the house had been agreed fifteen years ago after her wonderful mother had died leaving her money to start paying the mortgage. Then, out of her own teacher's salary she'd paid the monthly sum towards the twenty-year mortgage, faithfully continuing until she retired. She'd also tried renting to student nurses, teaching assistants, a librarian, but the young women found the kitchen and the bathroom shrouded in the dark ages. It was doing market research that rescued her – and with her pension she had managed. But now to re-mortgage, pay the arrangement fee... Flashes of pain rushed through her hip. Julia closed her mouth not to cry out as she edged into the living room.

The pain exhausted her. Having no energy was a trap and that fear was here. She must rest, but first she must appraise the room, find something of value to sell. Examining the closely knotted Persian carpet, she saw it was worn. Surely the oil painting of the old man with his donkey gathering firewood, would have value? But she had so wanted to leave it to Mike. He loved his home, always returned. Yes, Mike, he'll think of something. Of course he will, and assured she felt relieved. Slipping off her shoes, Julia lay down on the sofa, pulled up the crocheted rug.

I am opening the kitchen door to the yellow brick house. Mother is wearing her blue bathrobe and is at the kitchen table drinking a cup of tea, her hair a white cloud around her face. Startled, she gets up. 'Julia dear! What a lovely surprise! I thought you were up in Yorkshire teaching. Come in, dear.' My arm is around her and, for a moment, I rest.

Over the white porcelain sink, I see the dishes are filed there, as usual. In my left hand I hold the handles of a large straw basket.

Mother's mouth puckers. 'Did I forget you were coming, dear? My mind...I'm so sorry.'

'No, Mother. I've left the school. I'm not teaching now.' Her eyes open wide. 'Not to worry, it's something wonderful' and I hold out the basket.

'For me, dear?' Mother reaches out her hands, the joints swollen.

'Oh no, no, mine and Ian's. Sadly, he doesn't really want him.' I open wide the basket.

She bends over, a smile on her sun-wrinkled face. 'What a beautiful baby.'

'I'm forty. I've wanted a baby for so long.'

Mother's eyes read into mine. 'I know, dear. Who is Ian? Are you married?'

'Please understand, Mother, no man wants to marry me. Men only want to go to bed with me.'

She waits, then tilts her head. 'You have your baby and that is enough. Name?'

'Michael.'

'A strong name. I'll go up and make your bed. But first sit down. You must be very tired."

'You're not angry, disappointed?'

'No, no, dear. This is your home. The baby is your choice, your responsibility. It's wonderful to have you. Oh dear, I have a council meeting today and I must...'

'Wake up! Mum!'

Her eyes were tightly closed, but she knew Mike was standing by the sofa wearing his leather jacket.

'I've been calling and calling. How are you? It wasn't a bad drive from Manchester, the old Citroën didn't give out this time.' A loud laugh.

She opened her eyes, looked up at her son, tall, face thin, oh God, bald as a coot. A small sigh, then, 'Hello, darling. Lovely to see you.' A kiss from him on each cheek. 'Glad you woke me, I was dreaming ... Oh, the magic soup's ready, just light a flame.' And he was gone to the kitchen while Julia sat up, put on her shoes and followed him.

Stirring the soup, he said,. 'The tour went very well ... Very good reviews. Mostly full houses. Abroad, the Germans enjoy Harold Pinter. They like to be frightened. Soup is just what I need after a long drive. Nice to be home, great to see you.'

His beautiful head of red-brown hair, all gone! 'Bald ... Necessary for the part?'

'Yep. With luck, it'll grow back. Soup's hot. I'm starved,' and he served himself, sat in the chair.

'I've eaten,' and Julia cut slices from the loaf, sat next to him at the table. Of course she must wait to ask questions. He was very hungry. Probably tired from the show, then a long drive. Just enjoy watching his face, blue eyes, his jaws chewing ... She was very proud of the work she'd seen him do, but it was an uncertain life. The yellow brick house he loved, always connected it to his Nan. Two loving woman raising him. That was why he came here, to breathe in the world his grandmother had created – a home for all.

Mike's concentration was thorough, never a word until the bowl was wiped clean. Finished, he leaned back, let his hand run over his shaved head. 'Great, Mum. Poifect, as *The Sopranos* used to say. We played to good houses in the different university towns: Lille, Rheims, Strasbourg, Berlin, now back to Manchester. It's a hoot. A great company. We get along well. Just another two weeks to go and after that there are several days on 'Eastenders', a second reading for the RSC season. There's something else new, but first how are you?'

She said brightly, 'Everything's fine. My hip has been troubling me, but I'll see the doctor sometime. Oh, Cousin Jane comes next week and Lola is here for a short stay. Sends love. She's better, after an operation for gallstones. Now what else? You seem content.'

'I've met someone. Emily is the designer on the show. We're both going slow. Careful about repeating the past. She's a real sweetie.'

Julia felt her heart skip a beat, she'd seen this happen before. But she looked closely at her son, a glowing face. 'I'm so glad, Mike. I hope it works out well.'

'I've told her about the house, you, Nan. We'll drive down after the final performance, okay?'

She studied her swollen knuckles, then looked up. 'Wonderful. Just let me know when.' Yes, his entire self was happy.

'I'm sure you'll like each other. Now, how is the market research going? You seem to be doing more and more of it.'

'It's fine. I'm still going out every week but …' She stopped, the tightening of her stomach began again. 'We'll talk later. Emily?'

He stretched out his legs, looked up at the ceiling. 'Emily studied at Motley's, a wonderful, creative place and she is a minimal and brilliantly imaginative set designer. That's important for today, when there's little money. She's great fun.' He took a good breath and announced, 'We've decided to share a flat. A big step.' His face was becoming red.

Watching him with her heart, she thought how hard it is to speak to your mother about loving another woman.

'Emily has found a place near Finsbury Park. We'll sign the lease next week.' His eyes left the ceiling and he turned to her, smiling. 'It's not far from the station, easy for you to visit … '

She heard his decision and again fear came. What was she to do to save her house? Where was her help? A cold sweat spread down her back as she saw that he would leave her, that her home was going. She shrilled, 'There will be an increase in the mortgage payment on the yellow brick house.'

'What do you mean?'

'A 0.5% increase in the mortgage payment each month, starting January.'

He got up, started to pace up and down.

'One hundred and thirty-seven pounds a month more. It doesn't sound much.' Her words dribbled away.

'We both know it is.'

'It's only five years until the end of the mortgage,' she pleaded.

'Our flat's rent is seventeen hundred a month … If I'm not acting I'll do my usual decorating and electrics to pay my half. Friends are always asking me.'

'I can't do any more market research.'

'I didn't mean …'

'I don't think they'll extend the mortgage. I'm seventy-one.'

'I know.'

'I just received the letter.' She watched him moving, each hand in a fist. Offer some solution, she begged.

A furrow cut between his eyes. 'If I get a film, I'll be able to help. It's a real possibility.'

'I hope so, dear. But it may not happen … I could try to sell the house …'

The colour in his face went. 'Don't think like that! If we did that we'd be letting ourselves down, your mother, friends, relatives.'

'I'm trying my best.' Her helplessness made the words come out in a whine. 'I didn't mean to upset you tonight.'

'But you did.' He got up. 'Sell the family silver.'

'It's just plate. There's the painting.' In despair, she blurted out, 'Perhaps you could live here for a while, get a regular job.'

He stopped. As he looked into her face, his eyes became chips of ice. 'Do you know what you're asking, Julia? To put off Emily, give up my work – that is who I am, my life, can't you understand?'

'I'm sorry. I'm sorry,' Julia whimpered.

'They can't take the house from us. Our home. You welcome people here, that should be respected.' He was shouting, 'Oh shit, why are we so bloody helpless?'

'Please, Lola will wake.'

'It's our house – for almost a hundred years. That must mean something. We're not dreamers, like characters in *The Cherry Orchard*. You've worked and worked. I've always worked decorating, gardening, when not acting.'

'Please stop, dear. You're going to make me cry.'

'We'll find a way somehow. We will.'

Her voice was shaking. 'I'll speak to The Central Building Society. I'll keep on working as long as possible.'

'You'll have to, for the next five years. What a black joke!' He briefly put his arm around her.

'I'll ask the market research people. Please, let's not worry any further.'

'God, I'm bloody exhausted. I did two shows today, the drive. I need a drink.'

'There's just sherry, from last Christmas,' and opening the wooden cupboard she took out a bottle, poured it. She lifted her glass and with all her courage offered, 'A toast to you and Emily.'

As he drank, she saw he was afraid.

The sherry rubbed her throat. This was all she could give him tonight. She poured another drink. He refused. Not his thing – after the play, beer.

'I'm off to bed, Mum. Delicious soup. See you in the morning.' He hoisted his rucksack.

'I want you and Emily to be happy. That's what's important.'

'We will be and come to eat your magic soup at the yellow brick house.'

'Good,' and she ran her hand over his face, felt the prickly stubble of his beard. 'I'm out first thing, dear. If I'm not back by four, pop the shoulder of lamb in the oven, garlic, fresh rosemary, slow oven.'

Bending down, 'You're a real trooper, Julia.'

She listened to him going to his room. She must have faith that he'd find work: theatre, telly … Why not sell the picture of the donkey, a few hundred surely. Emily? A harbour for him. Be glad for him, as my mother was for me. If not, there'll be no future.

I'll turn out the lights now, go to bed, she decided. Tomorrow she'd finish the survey. As a teacher she understood the old cliché. She must try harder, do better.

The Home Boys

Mrs Cornwall pulled out the last squirt of milk, letting the cow's teats hang soft, the milk pail three-quarters full. She wiped down the udder again, carried the pail to the pasteuriser and emptied it, then washed it out.

'That's it, Becky.' The cow turned her head to look, switching her tail against the flies. 'It's not going to cool off, so take it easy.' Mrs Cornwall patted the rocky rump, then checked the feed and walked to the barn door.

The distant church bell was ringing five. She was in good time, Mr Cornwall would soon be back from the fields. As a treat the boy had been given a chance to pick berries today; after all it might be his last afternoon working on the farm.

Mrs Cornwall took off her glasses, wiped the sweat off the nosepiece and put them on again immediately. She needed glasses to see her way into the kitchen, although she'd been coming there for over twenty-five years. Of course she could see the large pieces of furniture, but the small things were near invisible. When she had time she liked sitting without glasses, rocking and looking at the blurred room. Now, there was a lot to do.

Mrs Cornwall bent down to fish in the sack for the potatoes that needed scrubbing. Tonight she'd planned to have the baked beans she'd made on Friday night, along with cold ham and greens with cherry pie for dessert. A good New

Hampshire Sunday evening meal. After that at around eight, Tom's mom and dad would show up to claim him. The crusts of earth fell off the potatoes into the sink, the running water breaking them.

Only three of them for dinner now, so there was no need to boil too many potatoes. Mrs Cornwall carried the aluminium pot to the stove, opened the door to put two logs on the fire. It was already three weeks since Chuck and Jerry had gone and now Tom'd had his fifteenth birthday. 'That's the way it always is,' Mrs Cornwall said. 'Get them from a Home at twelve: school, food, learn to farm, then at fifteen when they can earn a dollar, the mother and father come take them.' This was the fourth time she'd seen it happen, it was hard luck on her husband to manage the harvest without the three boys.

Was it twelve years since the first boys came, way back in 1935? They'd given up on having children; the Home Boys would give Mr Cornwall the extra hands he needed. But when the first three left, she remembered she'd felt annoyed at losing them. Now she didn't even remember their names. Chuck and Jerry were also fast disappearing. Tom's square face and uncombed hair popped up in her mind; she guessed she'd soon forget him too. The water was boiling and she emptied in the potatoes.

Outside the kitchen window she heard the tractor come up the yard, Mr Cornwall was driving to the barn. She went into the larder to get the food, then finished setting the table. Tom would be back now, he knew dinner was at six. She turned to open the kitchen door for her husband.

'I've finished the field. Next door gave me a hand otherwise I couldn't have done it,' Mr Cornwall said and bent down to unlace his boots. Pulling them off, he set them together then walked to the sink. The water spluttered from the faucet and he scooped it over his face and hair. Through half-closed eyes, he reached for the yellow soap to lather his hands and arms. 'Where's Tom?'

'He'll be here in a minute.' She heard the outside screen door snap shut. 'There, he knows it's dinner.'

Tom came in, balancing two overflowing pails. 'Evening, Sir, Ma'am. Sorry if I'm late.' He pushed the pails between them. 'I found tons of blueberries.'

Mrs Cornwall looked at them, then up at him. 'That's nice. It's almost time for dinner; put them in the larder and we'll go through them later.'

Tom stood undecided, waiting to say something.

'We're both ready, so you wash up,' said Mr Cornwall, putting on his slippers. They sat down.

After they'd finished the main course, Mrs Cornwall brought in the rest of the cherry pie and handed it around. 'What did you want so many blueberries for?' she asked.

'If you don't mind, Ma'am, I'm going to sell them.'

'In Concord with your Mom and Dad?'

'I've got my own pail, I want to make some money.'

'So do we all,' Mr Cornwall said.

'I want to try, that's all,' answered Tom.

'You've made up your mind about going then?'

In the pause they heard the sound of a motor revving up

the hill, tires scraping over stones, followed by the tattooing of a horn.

Mr Cornwall turned to the window. 'Good Lord, what's that?'

'I expect it's Tom's parents,' said Mrs Cornwall. 'They're early.' She went over to the window and was faced with headlights glaring at her. She closed her eyes. When she opened them the thankful dusk had returned and the car was quiet.

Tom stood beside her, his eyes shining. 'I didn't know they had a car.'

Mrs Cornwall looked into his face, then opened the kitchen door. She saw Tom's father waiting by the car. 'Good evening,' she said.

'Good evening, Ma'am. Sorry if we're early. We must've broke the speed record.' A woman was pushing herself out of the car. 'I'm Herb Bowen, Ma'am, and this is my wife, Delia.'

'Pleased to meet you.' Delia unstuck her dress, then held out her hand.

Mrs Cornwall came over, felt the rough palm against hers. 'Do come in.'

Mr Cornwall had turned back to finish his pie. He wiped his mouth. 'That must be a nippy car you've got.'

'My husband, Mr Cornwall.'

'How d'ya do.'

'Do sit down.'

Tom stood waiting by the stove.

'I can't sit down 'til I say hello to that boy of mine.' Smiling, Herb walked over. 'How ya doin', son?' and he patted him on the back. 'You're bigger than me, can you swallow that.'

Mrs Cornwall watched Tom as he looked at his father.

'Tom!' Delia moved slowly. 'I feel bad about not seeing you for three years, but I thought about you a lot.' She took his hand, put it to her cheek. His fingers curled into her face.

'Ya, we had a lot of problems. But I see you did okay without your Mom and Dad, and that's fine by me,' Herb laughed.

'Yes, he's a good boy. A natural farmer,' Mr Cornwall said.

'Ya, I bet.'

Delia smiled up at Tom, then put her arms around him. 'The others have all gone, but now my baby's coming home.' She pulled his head down and kissed him.

'Ya, Greg and Mike have vanished, but it'll be good to have you back.'

'He's a serious boy and hard working,' said Mr Cornwall.

Mrs Cornwall looked at her husband, nodded.

'That's good to hear. It's hard to find work but I heard they're looking for a sweeper at Schmidt's Sawmill. Five bucks a week. You'll go see them tomorrow, okay Tom?'

Mrs Cornwall went to pick up the coffee pot. 'Please sit down, have some coffee, pie.' She spoke quickly. 'Tom is able on the farm, also helps me in the vegetable garden. He likes that kind of work.'

'Ma'am, thank you, but we haven't time for coffee,' Herb said. 'We're in a bit of a rush. It's my brother's car and he wants it back tonight. So if you don't mind, Delia'd like to use the john and then we'll go.'

'Yes. Of course.' Mrs Cornwall stopped, looked over her shoulder, then led Delia to the hall.

'Tom, you'd better get your things together,' Herb said. 'And don't forget anything.'

'I want to ask Tom something before he goes,' interrupted Mr Cornwall.

'Sure. Why not? Since we're all preparing speeches, I want to say something too, when the ladies return.'

'I'd like you to stay on, Tom, if you could persuade your father.'

Around the door came Delia. 'What's that you said?' she broke in. Mrs Cornwall leaned against the wall.

'Take it easy, Deli. You're just in time for the birthday present we said we'd give Tom.'

Herb took out a crushed envelope and handed it to him. 'We're a little late for your birthday, but the thought's there anyway.'

Tom tore it open quickly. He unfolded a card, then fished out a single bill. He looked at it, gently smoothed it out. 'Five dollars.'

Mrs Cornwall heard the awe in his voice, saw his hand go through his hair making it stand up in all directions.

'Think we'd better go now, Herb,' Delia said. 'Do you need any help, Tom?'

'I'll be down in a minute, Mom.' He ran out and Mrs Cornwall could hear his feet racing up the stairs.

'Well, Ma'am, thanks again for all you've done for Tom. You'll hear from him at Christmas, I expect.'

'It was really nice to meet you both again,' Delia smiled. 'You'll be getting three new Home Boys in a couple of weeks to help you, I expect.'

Mr Cornwall got up and went to the sink for a glass of water.

'I'm ready,' Tom banged into the room with the suitcase. 'Thanks again, Ma'am, Sir.' And he took their hands, shaking them. 'Oh, Ma'am, do you mind if I take my pail of blueberries?'

'No, not at all,' Mrs Cornwall said, went into the larder and brought out the pail. 'Take it and Good Luck.'

He swung it up. 'Hey, Mom, you can make me a blueberry pie.' Delia and Herb followed him out.

Mrs Cornwall took the pie plates off the table and put them in the sink. Mr Cornwall was still standing.

'I think I'll go for a walk. It's hot.' He went into the hall for his walking shoes.

Mrs Cornwall stirred the suds around. 'Even fewer dishes tomorrow,' she said. 'That's a relief.' But then she thought the following week the new boys were coming. What were their names, she wondered. She dried her hands, opened the top drawer and found the Form Letter: Jack, Ned, Peter. She closed the drawer again, hung up her apron and sat down in the rocker. She took off her glasses, wiped them and looked around at the blurred room.

To be a Pilgrim

The bottle opener on his knife was worn, Luke noticed, as he prised off the cap on the litre of *Stella*. He'd controlled himself all morning, but now the liquid flowed quickly, easing his thirst, his mind. The beer, the racing movement of the car gave him a lift, and then a road sign whizzed past, the name of the town vanishing behind him. He should have read it. He'd promised to read the road signs for Jenny after they disembarked at Calais – just driving the old Citroën was all she could concentrate on and the only thing Peter enjoyed was looking at French maps. Now it was too late and they were dropping down the steep hill at speed.

'Sorry, Jenny, we've missed the turn-off. That was probably the sign to Vimy Ridge and the war monument, but my attention failed.' Luke squirmed against the pile of jackets, tins of Dulux paint, various bottles of wine and beer cartons sharing the back seat with him.

'Not to worry,' Peter called. 'I see from the map this road leads to the town of Vimy. At the top of this hill must be the Ridge, with the bomb craters from the First World War. We're a good way down now, so we'll keep on going to see what happens.' He lifted his glasses, looked at Jenny, patted her thigh. 'You're doing well, dear. Do keep remembering to drive on the right side,' and turned again to his map.

'For heaven's sake, you know I've been driving in France

for thirty years. I'm a better driver than you,' and she put her foot down on the accelerator.

Luke enjoyed hearing their family arguments. It was reassuring. Not like his own. He'd known Peter and Jenny for nearly twenty years, ever since he left art school, when they'd bought two of his graduation paintings. Since then he had decorated their house in Hampstead, and often came over from his council flat to cook a Chinese for them. Truth was, all he'd been able to do during the last few years was decorate houses, cook for friends and drink beer. He took another swallow, pressed the cap back on the bottle.

Looking at the back of Peter's head with its scattering of white hair, Luke said, 'You know the battle of the Somme has always been of interest to me. My father's older brother was killed there. As a boy I always wanted to come, and now you've made it possible. Grateful thanks to both.'

'The trip has worked well for us, too,' and Peter gave a wry smile. 'We're following the river Somme on the way to Mont Plaisir, our village. It marks a new adventure for me, as for all of us.'

Luke nodded. He knew Peter's early retirement from the university's archaeology department had been a serious disappointment, but there was nothing he could say to ease the loss. Instead, he'd concentrate on the scenery – the houses, the colour of the sun setting fire to the geraniums clustered in the window-boxes, note the blue wind blowing the net curtains into dark French rooms.

'Being on the road again is a gift. It's twenty years since I last left London to go abroad,' and Luke pulled hard on his ponytail. Yes, he'd spent half his life decorating other people's houses, earning money for Kate and for Rijn, their wonderful son. (And why shouldn't he call him after Rembrandt van Rijn, the greatest of painters?) Defiantly, Luke held up the half-empty beer bottle, a reminder of Hackney and the two up, two down where they once lived. The cap was off and he finished it. Bitter as the past.

Decorating all day, at night he transformed himself. A painter alone, he'd face the two-metre canvas waiting on the wooden easel down in the brick cellar. With a beer or several, he could free himself from the desolation of filling cracks in walls, rubbing down, applying Dulux, to concentrate on finding and awakening his other self. For years he had used the piercing light of a 150-watt bulb to illuminate the growing forms and geometric shapes that danced and whirled through his mind, and with his brush translated them onto his canvas. Over those years he applied careful strokes of vivid colour upon melting colour, until the objects he painted shimmered through their many layers, igniting their space.

Then one evening he stepped back, and it was there. The painting was as complete as possible. *Never ever truly finished,* said Francis Bacon – but it was his painting and after four years it was finished. Oh, the miracle, the shock of the moment. There had to be a beer to celebrate, and another one to find calm. Then even more bottles to hold the happiness, to temper fear. Of course he must give a salute to himself because it was he who had created the painting, finished it despite the decorating hell he'd experienced. And he soared higher and higher with the wonder and the beer. His painting coloured in beauty and pain was done, he shouted. He began to cry, mixed crying with shouting, and then he hit Kate because so much had gone into his commitment, the frustrating cost of loving her and Rijn. Also terror, for he'd looked deep inside for the next painting and couldn't see it.

How long he'd cried, been drunk, hit Kate and made her run away with Rijn, he couldn't remember. Afterwards, he wondered if finishing the painting had become an end of everything, a kind of death. He asked that often, while searching for a way to go on. And with the help of friends he managed to survive, to continue. Now in France, he was sitting in the back seat of Peter and Jenny's Citroën with sweat running down the side of his face. He wiped it off with his shirt-tail and closed his eyes.

'Luke, it's good to have you here with us. We're glad you thought of this detour to Vimy, a break before we start decorating the old house. It's the first time Jenny and I have gone to visit a war monument of this kind,' said Peter, and looking through the rear-view mirror realised that Luke hadn't heard a word. He picked up his map.

'I'm getting fed up,' Jenny announced. 'There's only this endless white line going down the hill. I'd really like to go back to the top, see Vimy Ridge. I'll look for a place to turn around.'

'Fine, love. No hurry. It's a pleasant ride. There's bound to be a spot sometime soon.'

Luke opened his eyes, the catnap had briefly rested his mind. He must try to let go of the past. After crossing the Channel this morning, he'd been renewed by the joy of seeing the French countryside, the furrowed dark brown earth stretching to the horizon. He'd seen the gently flowing River Somme, but there was nothing left to illustrate the battle. Yet on the nearby curving hill, Luke knew that phantom soldiers were still moving. Men forever heading towards the enemy – running, stumbling, falling. The black and white images rolled through his mind – pictures of voiceless, forgotten men. This vision needed to be explained, and again he leaned over Peter's seat. 'I think it's necessary to celebrate the men who fought here. Not their victory, but to make this a pilgrimage that recognises their commitment to each other, their comradeship.' But when he heard his words, they sounded trite, naff.

'You know, Luke, digging for artefacts from the ancient past has been my field, so I can understand your interest. I'm glad we can share our pilgrimage,' and Peter turned to smile at him. 'But, may I briefly change the subject and ask how the liver is doing?'

'Peter! No!' Jenny frowned.

'Going fast, Herr Professor. But have no worry, I'm not going to die on your hands, I promise.'

Yes, life and death was in balance, but there was a decision he could make today. 'I have good news. After three years of being frozen, I'm seeing a way through the painting block. With Kate and Rijn gone, my last painting unsold, I've decided to start again. So, cheers!' He reached for another bottle.

'You're painting again, that's wonderful,' Jenny said.

But he saw the disapproval in Peter's brown eyes when he slipped a half a litre in his trouser pocket. The Prof was getting old, didn't understand.

'Quick, Peter, there's a sign that says 'Little Vimy', I'm going to stop there,' Jenny said, and she swung the car across the road into a narrow street to stop by a clutch of sleepy houses. Opening the door, she stepped out into the sun, and stretching her arms took a deep breath, 'Oh, my dears, what a perfect day. Aren't we lucky!' A breeze caught loose strands of her hair. 'It's wonderful being here. What a relief to get out of the car.'

Peter pointed to a sign standing on the edge of a field. 'There's a Commonwealth Cemetery. Shall we go see it?'

'I'm not keen on cemeteries,' Luke said. 'Also my shoes have seen better days.' He looked down – a big toe wriggled through a hole in the blue canvas of his espadrilles.

'Luke dear, it's just a short walk. You said you wanted to come and we've been sitting for hours. We'll buy a new pair of shoes tomorrow at the supermarket, I promise,' said Jenny, putting her arm around his shoulder.

'All right, but I'm a townie and I shall walk at my own speed.'

She gave him a hug and, as Peter had started to follow the narrow path, hurried to catch up.

Luke marked the turnings of a gentle hill that passed by a field crowded with the first signs of green maize. Spring was earlier here, the earth different, firmer. He put his feet down carefully, for scattered along the way he recognised the rounded pieces of human bones. Red tinted, they were now part of the brick-red soil.

The path was dry, but alongside it a gully had been formed by the winter rain pouring down from the ridge high above. Luke tilted his head way back to look at the vertical slope leading to the far distant tree line. That must be Vimy Ridge, where land met the sky. He followed the long lip around the curving earth. It made him dizzy, seeing the edge of the ridge hanging over him.

Didn't a hundred thousand men die here? And as he looked, the spring trees seemed to turn into a landscape of mud and men. Bodies falling. Theirs. Not his. Not a true comparison, but he couldn't help making it. Arms flailing, legs twisting. He could hear men shouting, 'Stretchers! Stretchers!' And he cried out, 'Comrades, you know loneliness, pain. Is it possible to blow life into the dying?' Luke listened and hearing silence his hand reached in his pocket, felt the cool shape of the *Stella*. No. No.

He could no longer look at the Ridge, instead he must find a different scene to block his fear. At the end of a sentry line of poplars were Jenny and Peter. They were standing in the dappled sunlight, creating a country picture of two loving people. Nearby was the Little Vimy cemetery where each marble headstone rested on a green grave.

Jenny began to wander along a row. She stopped from time to time to shake her head. 'They are Canadians, so young ... eighteen ... twenty-one ... twenty-three ...'

'Mostly Scottish names – Alastair MacDonald … James Grant … David Hooper,' Peter said. 'All with a cross – their names and dates carved in the stone.'

Luke walked by the graves, each the same length, width. Ordered respect for the disordered dead. He had reached the furthest corner of the cemetery when he saw there were three separate graves, set apart. He approached slowly and found two headstones with crosses, but without names. 'Here Lies A Soldier Known Only To God,' he read.

Then he went over to the last headstone. It stood by itself – bore the name L. Shearer. But there was no cross, no dates. Who was this man whose birth and death no God knew? A man alone, known only to himself. Using his hand, Luke brushed the stone name free of dust.

'Of course, I recognise you,' Luke said, opening the *Stella*. Holding it high, 'You were an artist like me.'

The Ladies Play Poker

'Christa!' Greg called. He was coming towards her. 'Shall we dance?' he asked in his husky voice, his body tall and strong.

In a moment she was in his arms, swaying to the refrain of an old song, "It's a sin to tell a lie." Suddenly she felt his mouth gently brushing her cheek. In response she raised her lips to meet his. They touched and the world was heaven for her. In that moment, Christa knew that he loved her, and that she loved him...This was the truth.

Dora closed *True Love Magazine*. She looked at the cover with the beautiful woman, her smiling blue eyes, her perfect golden hair, and felt ashamed. At forty-four she read love stories – other people's romances. Even her young niece asked why she read them, but she couldn't get the words together to tell her about every day on 87th Street and West End Avenue. She couldn't explain the cleaning, the cooking for the family, and that in the evenings Uncle Harry was tired after managing ten Carlton Drug Stores, so he often shouted at dinner. After that, all he could do was fall asleep over *The Post* newspaper. Each day she was missing something; what it was she wasn't sure. But, God forbid, she wasn't complaining about her home!

She looked around at her large bedroom, the sun coming through the open windows. A nine-room apartment, large enough for the people she loved most in the whole world, and all of them living together. First of all there was Momma, then her sister Gretel and her two little girls, as well as her Harry and their grown-up Deena and Ruthie. Her family. Still, she couldn't stop herself from reading *True Love Magazine.* Dora sighed as she put it on the bedside table, straightened the candlewick bedspread. Housework done, the chicken boiled, so the day was free. What should she do?

Looking out through the window at the ledge of the apartment building opposite, she saw that the New York sun had already baked dry the new pigeon droppings. It was going to be a hot day for June, impossible for the hairdresser. At the dressing table, Dora put the comb through her wavy brown hair and quickly dabbed on her lipstick. The down powder-puff she enjoyed the most, it tickled, made her laugh, as the perfumed powder whitened her nose.

Her sister Gretel always gave her things that smelled good. Gretel, whom she loved best of all her three sisters – the smartest, working hard and making lots of money, even paying most of the rent for the large apartment. But not so smart with men. Too bad she didn't love Leon Goodman any more. So handsome. A man of culture. A gentleman. A rich man's son but after the terrible bank crash in 1933, a bankrupt. Dora shook her head at the memory. And Gretel, now divorced, was breaking her heart over that rich David Klein, who had a wife already. Lonely Gretel with her two girls, her swansdown powder puffs, and Dora sighed.

The clock chimed. Eleven o'clock already, and still no

decision what to do. Looking at herself in her flowered dress, Dora saw that she needed a new brassière. Yes, she'd go down to Orchard Street, visit her sister Debbie's undergarments shop. So she put on her blue straw hat with the cherries, picked up her handbag and at that moment the phone rang. Immediately she thought of the family – who's sick? Jenny? Max? Debbie?

'Dora speaking. Who is it? What's the matter?'

A woman's voice said, 'Hello, Dora. How are you? How's Harry and the girls? Don't you recognise my voice? It's Essie, Essie Brookes from the old days in the Bronx, don't you remember?'

Dora remembered, but why was she phoning? She recalled last seeing Essie five years ago at a wedding shower, and they hadn't talked. They'd stopped being friends years ago when her Jake made a lot of money opening up a fur shop on Fifth Avenue, leaving Allerton Avenue far behind.

Essie spoke quickly. 'I know it's a long time, but I've been thinking of you and it would be wonderful to see you. It's short notice, but why not meet today?'

Dora didn't have time to answer as Essie said, 'Can you believe it, but right now I'm at Ida Kaye's apartment. You know Ida Kaye, Bernie Kaye's mother? Bernie Kaye, the famous comedian. At Grossinger's he made me laugh so hard, I almost peed in my pants. Well, Ida lives at 135 East 72nd Street, off Park Avenue, and the ladies were just ready to have a game of poker when one of the gang phoned to say she couldn't make it. Four could play, of course, but one more would be better. So why not come over now, Dora? Five cents a point, a friendly game and it would be wonderful to hear about Harry and the girls.'

Dora's head was spinning. 'Essie, please hold the wire for a minute so I can think.' A poker game with new faces. Five cents a point was a lot, but why not see her again? 'All right, I'll come. I don't know Ida or Bernie Kaye, but I'd like to hear about your Jake and Jerry. 135 East 72nd Street?' And she put down the phone.

A big decision. She opened the little drawer in the bedside table. Her special purse was hidden there, holding the dollar bills that Harry didn't know about, all saved from the weekly housekeeping money. She took out twenty dollars, the most she could afford to lose. She'd forget about the brassière.

Dora took the 86th Street cross-town bus and transferred down Lexington. The heat was already making her dress stick to the seat, so she moved delicately around to free it. Her nerves were bothering her too, making her wonder if she'd made a mistake coming to the East Side. But why should she worry about Essie Brookes after having shared a two-family house for seven years?

She got off the bus at 72nd street and around the corner saw the apartment number. A building with a canopy and a doorman in a green uniform who showed her inside, told her to wait while the apartment was buzzed. The hall had shiny furniture, low tables with flowers in vases, mirrors brightly lit by hidden bulbs. Dora shuffled nervously back and forth in the chair, then heard her name announced.

THE LADIES PLAY POKER

Leaving the elevator at the twelfth floor, she found the apartment door open, and entering the hall she suddenly felt arms around her. Ida Kaye's red lips welcomed her, and it was evident that she'd recently been to the hairdresser – her gold-blonde hair was perfectly sausage-curled high on top of her head.

'Glad to meet you, Dora. You are a doll to come,' Ida smiled. 'Food there's plenty of, so take your hat off, sit down, eat, make yourself at home.'

Dora took off her hat and left it on a table in the hall and followed Ida into the living room. And there stood Essie Brookes, enormous, arms open. Dora was engulfed and the sweet Essie smell from the past poured over her.

'I've gained weight – chocolates. But what the hell,' she laughed. 'You look good, a couple of wrinkles more, but who's counting,' and holding on to the back of the bridge chair she sat down. Then Essie reached over to an open box of candy on the card table, took a handful of chocolates and dropped them in her mouth. 'You sit next to me,' she said, chewing. 'I don't always play, mostly come for the chocolates.' And pulling a chair over, she turned to the woman near her, 'You don't mind, for an old friend? Dora, this is Mary. She's a sharp poker player, remember that.'

After sitting down, Dora turned to look into two large blue eyes. 'How do you do?' she managed.

'Why the hell are you frightening her? I'm a good-hearted slob and you know it,' Mary said smiling, showing perfect teeth. 'I'm from Canada. I see you like flower dresses. I've got cotton dresses of real good cotton. Best English quality. Also blouses. I'll show you, I've got some here. A special price.' She started to get up.

'Wait a minute, Mary,' Ida interrupted. She was holding a plate in her hand. 'Let Dora have some lunch, we want to begin the game now.' She put the potato salad, pastrami, pickles, rye bread on the table in front of Dora.

'Also, she hasn't met the other ladies yet. You'll have plenty of time to sell your schmatas later,' and pointing to the woman on the opposite side of the table Ida said, 'This is Brownie Fox.'

Dora looked across and saw a round-faced lady wearing a necklace of diamonds and emeralds as big as the potatoes she was eating.

'Next to her in the pearls is Gladys Fisher, the wife of a lawyer.' Ida looked around the table: 'Everybody meet Dora Caine.'

The ladies smiled at her. Dora nodded back, her mouth full as she tried to eat quickly. She saw that they were in a hurry to begin – the cards were already out, piles of stacked chips in front of all the ladies, the score pad set and Ida busy writing the names of the players in ordered margins. When she stopped eating for a moment, a maid appeared who asked quietly if she was finished. Dora looked into her black face, at the neat cotton frill pinned in her hair, and handed her the plate.

'Five card poker, Jokers wild, five cents a point, twenty-five cents to play,' Ida announced and cut the deck. She turned to Brownie on her left, who also cut for dealer. Ida won.

A good hand, could be a full-house, Dora thought, holding her five cards close. She agreed to twenty-five cents to stay in the game, taking two cards from the pack and throwing away one. Is it worthwhile to stay in with two eights, a jack and two threes? She looked around – Ida and Brownie were out. Gladys and Mary were carefully rearranging their hands. Dora decided to stay in for another twenty-five cents and asked for one card. They played until Mary called for five dollars. Dora knew that Mary couldn't do better than two eights and two threes, she must be bluffing. Dora paid the red chip, carefully put her cards down on the green felt. Mary laid out a five-card straight flush.

'Sorry, dear,' Mary said. 'I got a rosie blouse that'll really suit you.'

'Lucky in cards, unlucky in love,' Essie winked at Dora, and took several chocolates.

'You should talk, Tootsie,' answered Mary. 'Jake never even bothers to come home to your fancy-schmancy apartment on Park Avenue. We're both married to shits; the only difference is that yours is rich.'

Dora sat not knowing what to think or do. Ida was already dealing out a new hand. Not only were there the cards to consider, but the news about Essie's husband was upsetting. Jake was absent. Her Harry snored and shouted but never wandered – did that make her lucky? She picked up the cards and saw they were bad. Better be careful after the last mistake. She could only manage a few more hands if she kept on losing.

Dora and Gladys passed. Brownie and Ida were in with Mary. Ten, fifteen dollars and they still bid on. Sweat was dripping from Essie's temples as she ate more chocolate, and Brownie put her Swiss cotton handkerchief down her dress front and dabbed between her breasts. 'God, this weather is killing,' she said and raised the ante another ten dollars. There was over a hundred dollars in the pot when Ida called.

Dora lit a cigarette to steady her nerves. Fortunately Gretel had given her a pack and, holding the Camel with her thumb and two fingers, she sucked in the smoke and watched the cards being laid on the table. Mary won again with a full house.

'You're in top form, Mary,' Ida said.

'Yeah.'

Brownie took off her blouse, and laid it on the back of the chair. 'Sorry, I gotta take it off,' she said. Her breasts were encased in an all-in-one corset. Dora recognised the quality.

'It's new,' Brownie said. 'But I can't breathe. There's no air in this room. It's a nice apartment, Ida, but you need cross-ventilation. Thank God I'm going to Europe in two weeks and will miss the summer.' She lifted up her emerald and diamond necklace, mopped under the stones, then again between her breasts.

Mary turned to Gladys. 'What's the matter? You're not talking. Your husband busy at the office day and night?'

'You know Martin,' said Ida. 'Goes to bed with a book.' She started dealing a new hand. 'You in?'

Dora nodded and gathered the new cards. Ida put the pack down and turned a six of clubs over. Dora needed it. I could win this game, and took a last puff from Gretel's cigarette. Now, I got tip-top cards. With a bit of luck I'll get the nine of clubs as well, she thought, and saw Mary discard the nine.

'Five dollars to stay,' Ida said.

Dora agreed and picked up the two cards, tried not to let her face show hope. The ante was put up and missing only one card for a straight, Dora paid. She picked a Joker from the pack and called for ten dollars. She'd won! She, Dora from West End Avenue had beaten them, all these smart ladies. A bubble of laugher rose from inside, and Dora looked around as Ida shuffled and dealt a new hand.

'Your husband going with you to Europe, Brownie?' said Gladys.

'You kidding? He says he'll meet me in Cannes in July; I don't believe him.' She turned to Mary. 'Charlie's still got hot pants for your husband's ex-wife, and only wants to meet up with her.'

'What do you want from me? Gretel's still stuck on that rich David Klein, so tell Charlie to forget it,' and Mary asked for three cards.

'How do you know?' Brownie demanded.

'Don't wet your stones. All these years Leon still owes David Klein money, so he hears them talking when he goes up to his office. I don't even know Gretel, but I know she's going to Paris with David Klein,' said Mary, then turned to Ida, 'Raise you ten dollars.'

Dora felt her face pricking red. What is Mary talking about? Was it possible that this Mary has something to do with David Klein and Gretel's ex-husband, Leon Goodman? Oh, my God! She put the cards down. 'Not in,' Dora managed to say and looked at Mary arranging her cards. Leon's new wife is talking about my sister Gretel, his ex-wife. She looked at Essie, who was busy choosing another chocolate. The ladies are chewing on Gretel like lox and cream cheese on a bagel, thought Dora. I'll stop them, I'll tell them who I am. But her hands were shaking in her lap.

Brownie called for twenty dollars, then waved her cards. 'I win. A full house against your bluff. Mary Goodman, you're slipping. Are you jealous that Leon's carrying a torch for Gretel?'

'Cut the crap, Brownie, it's you whose face is green.'

This was the moment to speak, and Dora took a breath, 'Ladies, I want you to know I'm Gretel Goodman's sister.'

Silence. All the eyes bored holes in her.

'Here you are, Mrs Kaye – coffee and cake,' said the maid, opening the door and placing a silver cake plate on the table. 'I hope the cheese cake is as good as it looks,' she said pushing in the coffee trolley. 'You ladies all enjoy yourselves.'

The only sound was of cake being eaten. Dora watched while the ladies sank their teeth into the cheese cake and Ida totalled the losses, the gains of the game.

Then Mary leaned over, put a hand on her arm. 'No offence meant, Dora. You know that Gretel of yours is quite a smart cookie.' Dora nodded. 'She must be if she left Leon.

Tell her that from me. I'm the only schmuck that would have married him. I make the money. He takes me nowhere, don't bring in a dime.'

Dora felt her arm go numb. 'I'm sorry to hear that, Mary. But as God is my witness, maybe he couldn't pay his bills but he always took Gretel to the best places, treated her like a queen.'

'Believe me, when we go to Canada, I pay. He gets the best English jackets up there. Nothing too good for the big shot bankrupt from the Goodman family, but look for a job? No, he's too proud for that,' Mary said, letting go of her arm.

Of course there was more to Leon Goodman than a bankrupt and Dora couldn't stop the words rushing out, 'Mary, when Leon had money he went to theatres, museums, concerts with Gretel. He speaks three languages, used to play golf at the Country Club. He reads books, *The New York Times*. Not just a bankrupt. A gentleman.' Dora sank back in her chair, her throat scraped dry.

'Listen! Ladies!' Ida interrupted. 'Mary's the winner for two hundred and thirty-six bucks. The next is Dora, who is ahead of the game for forty dollars. The rest of us got to pay up,' and Ida passed around the slips.

The dollar bills were crisp when Dora folded the money into her handbag. Brownie said that next week was her last game, but Ida and Gladys would still be playing for three more weeks, that Essie and Jerry were going to Maine.

'You certain you don't want a summer blouse with flowers?' Mary said. 'I'll show you,' and holding Dora by the arm led her to the hall. 'This is pure one hundred per cent cotton,' she said and opening a bag held up a white blouse with tiny red roses. 'Take it. It's yours, it'll suit,' and Mary gave it to her.

Dora held it up, felt it, then started to speak, but Mary had already gone back inside. Holding the blouse she followed her in, and all the ladies turned to look at her. What should she say? Seeing the lonely faces, she cleared her throat, 'I just want to say thank you for a very nice game. Essie, it was good to see you. And it was really nice meeting all of you ladies.'

She returned to the hall, put on her hat, and before closing the door behind her, put the rosie blouse on the hall table.

Always Peaceful in Mont Plaisir

The boys in his form at the Lycée whispered the word *pédé*, poofter, to Jean-Pierre as he left the classroom. Then a line of hairy teenagers climbed onto the school bus behind him, their sheep mouths baa-ing at his bottom. Also Georges and Christian, two boys from his own village thought it funny to keep crowding him further into the school bus, and after bursting into loud laughter collapsed onto empty seats. Two girls, Antoinette and Claire, also stepped onto the bus, their heads bent in embarrassment as they sat down. Had they heard the word? Of course, and Jean-Pierre's face became even a brighter pink because Antoinette, who sat near him in class, used to be a friend and often came over to play with his little sister. No, no, it wasn't his fault that, like a girl, he hadn't hair on his face or body, although he'd be seventeen tomorrow. Low red blood cells meant the hair hadn't grown, nor had his voice changed. The cause was his illness, the doctor said. But when he was told about being slow to *passe la puberté*, he hadn't really understood how strange looking he'd be. How could he explain that to the stupid boys?

Moving to the back, he stumbled over the satchels and rucksacks thrown helter-skelter in the aisle. His legs were like noodles and in his trousers his *zizi* had shrivelled up like a wizened carrot. Holding his rucksack in front of his body, he sat down on the furthest bench.

Was it only a week ago that he'd joined the Sixth Form? What a shooting star moment that had been – to get on the bus and begin his studies at the Lycée Victor Hugo, a high school with a library near the great Cathédral of Laon. His yellow hair, pink and white face made him look like a rabbit, but why think of that when he could meet with other students, have a friend – instead of being ill and taught at home? Yet, after two days he saw the bright star falling into shit. *Pédé*, then *crevette*, rent boy, were whispered at him as he walked into the school hall. Going down the echoing school steps, voice after voice took up the words, passing the sentence that he was 'a bum boy'. Sex – he hadn't thought much about it and to have a girlfriend looking as he did, how could that happen? As for love – he loved his mother and his little sister Élodie, but his scrounging older brother, he barely spoke to. Now, sitting next to the back window, he tucked in his legs, using up as little space as possible.

The school bus followed the curve of the serpent road, letting off pupils at the different stops. This ride he'd once enjoyed, passing by harvested fields dotted with round bales of straw, then through small villages of grey stone houses with pots of red geraniums set carefully on the window-ledges. But today he let it all go by and sat with closed eyes, only opening them occasionally to see where they were.

He squinted as the bus entered his once favourite village – Éboulou. Here was the little dell filled with a weeping willow tree and, in its centre, the plaster statue of the Virgin Mary wearing her sky blue veil of purity. Smiling gently, she held out a blessing in her delicate hand. A week ago it seemed to be for him and that had made him laugh with happiness. But what a stupid mistake! Today he knew the truth. It was a load of shit to think that he was included in her love when she, like most people, must have contempt for him. Her presence today only held a warning – that he was different and must hide his true feelings.

It was clear no one would understand him, especially his mother. She'd be shocked at the ugly names he was called at school, lift her hands to her face, her eyes looking at him in panic. Then she'd insist he stay at home forever. Her daily litany would begin – I work hard, so why has this terrible thing happened to Jean-Pierre? I keep everything in order, why can't Bernard keep a job? Why can't the Patron promise my husband agricultural work until he retires? Then she'd find her answer in the white pills in a bottle hidden in the bathroom cupboard. They silenced her, allowed her to sleep and finally gave the family peace.

The bus bumped in and out of potholes as he imagined his mother in the kitchen stirring the soup. In her way she tried to do her best for him, protect him with her suffocating care. And tomorrow she'd celebrate his seventeenth birthday and say, 'You are almost *un adult*.' But wasn't it up to him to decide what he was?

The final stop was at Mont Plaisir, his home, and Jean-Pierre decided to remain seated until the bus was parked in its set place behind the red-brick church. While the driver filled in the time sheet he waited, watched what Georges and

Christian were going to do. They started down the steps, but at the bottom they turned and in unison shouted the ugly word at him before running away. Antoinette waited, kept looking at him, then she jumped from the steps and also ran off. At last he could go.

Standing on the road, his rucksack felt heavy, as if filled with lead. And there, like a spectre arising from the graveyard, was Madame Chevalier walking down the cemetery path towards him. Her busy spinster nose ready to sniff into everybody's business, if she'd heard the word spoken by Georges and Christian. The thought of all the village knowing made his stomach rise to his throat. Then Madame Chevalier stopped in front of him and he struggled to hide his nausea.

'Bonjour, Jean-Pierre. A good day at school, eh?' Her yellow teeth showed as she smiled.

'Oui, merci, Madame Chevalier,' he mumbled.

'But it's always nice to return home. Toujours le calme à Mont Plaisir, isn't that so?' She gave him a bigger smile.

'Oui, Madame. It's always peaceful here,' he swallowed, his face cracking. Then with 'Good-day, Madame,' he fled in the direction of his father's house.

But before reaching the safety of home, he had to pass the Patron's house with its huge barn. Outside, a monster was parked there – the mammoth yellow and green John Deere combine harvester that his father drove. Towering above the roof of the Patron's house, the gross machine looked down on him, challenging him to scale it, drive it like a man to the fields. He knew it was a job he could never ever do. What then would be his future, he worried as he ran to his house, opened the door.

His mother stopped stirring the soup and came over to welcome him with a kiss on both cheeks. 'Feel well? Everything all right? Good. Wash your hands. Dinner is ready,' then she returned to the large wood burning stove. 'Your father is hungry and he is working tonight on the tractor.'

'I know. Sorry I'm late.'

At the head of the kitchen table sat his father, chewing on the rounded end of a baguette; field dust filling the lines in his face. Élodie sat next to him, and she waved, while Bernard was looking at the pictures in his girlie magazine.

'Slow poke, Jean-Pierre,' Élodie sang.

'I had to stop and talk to Madame Chevalier.'

'Yes. 'Toujours le calme',' his mother said, lifting the pot of soup and setting it in front of his father, next to the boiled potatoes.

The smell of Friday dinner soothed Jean-Pierre, and the comfort followed him as he went to wash. A smell of hope, of family, but it couldn't stop the fear that gnawed at him. Only half-day at school tomorrow, still he must again face the accusations. He went into the bathroom and after washing decided to look inside the cupboard. How fortunate, his mother's bottle of calming pills was almost full. He would think hard, decide what to do with them, then closed the cupboard and went inside.

He wasn't hungry. Instead with his fork he moved the bits of carrots, onions, turnips, the fatty meat, and tried to avoid his mother's questioning eyes. Talk would start only when his father finished eating his soup. Of course his father was hungry, driving the harvester from seven until five, then out again until midnight. Jean-Pierre watched his earth-stained fingers push the bread around the sides of the bowl, then he caught the crust, shoved the dripping piece in his mouth, swallowing it.

After licking his fingers his father leaned back in his chair, 'We'll finish harvesting the sugar beet tonight, a good crop. Next year the bastards at the EEC will cut down on the beet. Too much grown. Less sugar needed. They want to close down the refining factories. Next year, the year after, it'll be finished, then what will happen?'

No one answered. Bernard looked up from his magazine. 'I'm out tonight, going to a disco.'

His mother leaned over to him, 'Any news about your interview for the job in Éboulou? Keeping the streets clean, the verges tidy, is worthwhile.'

'It's too far to go,' Bernard said.

'You could bicycle there.'

'I'm waiting to hear.'

Now she turned, 'How is school, Jean-Pierre?'

'All right. I've lots of homework to do.'

'Any new friends?'

'Maman,' Élodie interrupted, 'I saw Antoinette yesterday. She's in Jean-Pierre's form and says –'

'It's no one's business what anyone says,' he shouted.

'You're silly,' and Élodie made a face at him.

'Why aren't you eating?' his mother asked.

He shrugged his shoulders. 'I have a bad stomach.'

'I'll get something for it. Tomorrow is your birthday. I haven't forgotten. An important date. We'll have a cake.'

'I don't want to be seventeen.'

'You're supposed to be the smart one, think you can stop time?' laughed Bernard.

'Be quiet, ignoramus.'

'Let's see you try, ugly,' and Bernard got up. 'See you later.' He ran his fingers through his dark hair, opened the kitchen door and striding out rattled the coffee cups on the sideboard.

His father finished the wine, wiped the drops on his chin. 'Three more years, then I retire. Never to go out on the harvester again.' His sun-tired eyes squinted at them. 'You know what will happen then? The government will want to cut my pension,' and shoving back his chair, he got up. 'Forty years working in the fields. Three thousand hectares the Patron and I harvest.'

No need to say anything, Jean-Pierre thought, we've heard this moan a hundred times.

His father got up, picked up the bag of sandwiches and bottle of water on the table. Before opening the door he turned to Jean-Pierre, 'Understand, there'll be no work for you in Mont Plaisir.'

His mother said nothing, only stood in the doorway watching his father walk into the night. Then she closed the door, went to the sink. Jean-Pierre took the plates over, scraped the remains into the pail, wiped the table.

Élodie opened a box of coloured beads, turned to Jean-Pierre. 'Shall I make you a special present for your birthday?'

'I don't need any stupid present.'

'Why speak to your sister like that? It's not nice,' his mother said, frowning.

'Leave me alone,' he said and picked up his rucksack.

'You're horrid. I won't make anything for you, but I'll make a lovely pink flower for Maman.'

'Thank you, dear, I'd like that,' his mother said, leaning over the earthenware sink.

Going into the room he shared with his brother, Jean-Pierre dropped the rucksack on his bed. Usually, he'd take out his books and go back in to study at the kitchen table. He liked to half-listen to Élodie's chatter about animals she would imagine playing with – donkeys, penguins, baby elephants. But tonight his head was filled with shadow thoughts. He looked around at the room. The usual mess of Bernard's clothes heaped on the floor, his after-shave cologne still stinking the air. He never wanted to look at his brother's side of the room, the pictures on his wall, the things he was always busy watching. Most days they hardly spoke. He had nothing to say to him.

Now he decided to kneel on Bernard's bed and look. The wall facing him was crowded with glued on magazine and newspaper cut-outs of smiling girls with only a few bits of clothing on. And there, stuck in the lowest corner nearest Bernard's pillow, were two photos of women all undressed – big breasts, red nipples and legs spread so wide apart you could see the hole. He'd watched Bernard having a game with his zizi with them, heard him groaning, shouting, shaking. Afterwards Jean-Pierre felt funny, upset. There were also photos of rock stars: The Rolling Stones, Prince and blonde, half-naked Madonna, all English-speaking. Stupid Bernard didn't understand a word, while he did.

Jean-Pierre sat down on his own bed. He looked at his wall. Alongside his bed was the picture he'd chosen ... A steep broken cliff and below, standing alone on the sand, a man with his back to him, looking out to sea – a few footprints on a beach with rolling, foaming waves coming in. The colours of the sea and sky were different shades of blues and greys. It was a place far away, and he'd never been there. Looking again, he thought there's something wrong with my picture. What, he didn't know. Yet he knew the thing that did for Bernard, wasn't for him. But what was it that he wanted? He carefully went over that question and found that nothing made him shout aloud. There was a gap in his heart. To want nothing was to be finished, dead.

Both Bernard and his father would be out late. He could take seven of his mother's pills – no one would notice. If he started to wake up early in the morning he could take more, that would complete everything. The thought made his hands cold, his heart go faster ... He must be strong when he went through the waiting, when he became sleepy. If he concentrated on his uselessness, that would help. There was nothing here for him, that was the trouble. He would go on being as he was, making everyone sick. How wonderful not to have anyone making fun of you ever again, to always have peace.

Jean-Pierre reached under his pillow for his pyjamas, put them on. Now he'd wash, and went into the kitchen. The television was on – a woman in front of a clock was speaking. His mother was watching, then turned to him in surprise. 'What are you doing, Jean-Pierre?'

'I'm tired. I thought I'd go to bed early.'

She got up, went up to him and put her hand to his forehead. 'No fever. Good. Goodnight.' She smiled and kissed him. 'Be nice and say goodnight to Élodie.'

His sister held up a long thread, on it were shiny pink and rose coloured beads. 'Aren't they pretty?' she said.

He watched her add a red bead. 'What are you making?'

'A beautiful heart.'

'For me?'

'Of course, silly Jean-Pierre.'

A Prize

Holding the strap in the bumpy jumpy underground train, Doris couldn't help thinking now her sixtieth birthday was nearing what it meant to be a winner. In the *Metro* newspaper, in *The Evening Standard,* and especially when she glanced over the shoulder of someone reading *Hello*, there were always stories, pictures about wonderful, successful people. But to her, the real meaning of finding success or gaining a prize was very difficult to understand. As she thought about her life's work, all that would amount to were many years of completing the monthly statement of accounts for the customers of the *Eastern Building Society.* Was doing that job most of your life any sign of success, or of being a prize winner? She had to laugh.

But she mustn't forget that in May, thirty-five years ago, she had won something. She'd been loved by and been married to Derek. He was a builder and together they'd scraped together enough money to pay the down payment on a small house in the new, green Milton Keynes. But on a late December afternoon two years later, everything had been lost. Derek was killed on the building site where he worked, after slipping and falling from the scaffolding. Her parents and her brother Edward, who lived in New York, came to stay for a week in her and Derek's house. They offered her kind words, but for her the world was empty. Finally, she found the courage to sell the house, then moved to London to start her new job with the *Eastern Building Society*.

Since then, today and every day, she tidied her rented flat on Black Horse Road and walked down into the Underground to go to work. Not a long ride to Highbury and Islington, but as always there were people crushing against her. Today a swinging backpack just missed hitting her head, so why not shut out the crowded train, think about prizes in her childhood?

One early sun-filled day she, her parents and brother Edward went on the ferry to the Isle of Wight. Walking along the Chine she held her breath to see the wild waves coming in, then going head over heels and breaking far below. After that excitement they all went to a pub with a garden of roses where her brother and she had a Coca-Cola and also entered a history quiz being held there. The special moment came when Edward, who was eleven, won the prize money because he knew who the Prime Minister was in 1935. But the best part was that with the five shillings he bought her a vanilla dairy ice-cream cornet. Yes, it was then that she and Edward had been encouraged to believe that winning a prize was important. Their father, who left school at fourteen, was eager for them to do well and began to repeat, 'You must always try to win'.

At the time, the family was living in a council house in Haringey, two up, two down, a brown tiled coal fireplace in the living room. After French-polishing furniture all day, father would arrive home, take off his coat, and wash his hands for tea, although they never really became white clean. Then, after beans on toast and his cup of tea, he'd look over their arithmetic papers, their English sentences, quiz their spelling and if either she or Edward made a mistake, he'd give that person a hard smack.

'You must learn,' he challenged. 'If there is a prize going, you must win it.'

She did try, but even so there were many smacks for her, especially when she was alone and Edward was at the Grammar School. His name always headed the Honours List and at graduation he and father received loud cheers and congratulations.

There was no surprise when she went to Haringey Secondary Modern. The English teacher, Miss Golding, let her write stories – spooky tales about policemen and gangsters, but sometimes she made up stories about animals. Words came springing out of her mind – a story of a beetle, who first found a home in a little girl's raggedy slipper. *A crusty brown beetle with long waving antennae, who also liked to explore pockets – discovering cigarettes in the boy's, not a shilling in the mother's, but in the little girl's a note with magic stick signs on it that had to be deciphered by the beetle and which led to* ... And although Doris hadn't quite finished her story, she handed it in. She remembered vividly that when the going home bell rang, Miss Golding said, 'Doris, please stay behind a moment.'

A dark feeling grew inside her when she stopped by the teacher's desk. The room was silent with the last of the children gone. Her mind buzzed with worry as she waited for Miss Golding to finish the week's register. But when she looked up, Miss Golding was smiling at her.

'Doris, I like your story. Please finish it by tomorrow. It's the best story in the class. You have a delightful imagination,' she said and reached over to pat Doris's hand.

Doris stood there, fingers twisting her hair, her heart bumping.

Miss Golding pulled open her desk draw. 'Staying so late, would you like a sweet, a Mingles Chocolate?' and she gave her one.

Holding the shiny green paper tightly in her hand, Doris started to run towards her home. Should she tell her father? Was it important that her teacher liked her story? Of course she'd finish it by tomorrow, but one sweet wasn't really a prize, was it? So, she decided not to say anything to anyone.

The train came to a stop. Not possible to hold memories going to work, she thought. Just then the young man turned, the backpack came swinging at her. 'You're a prize idiot with your stupid backpack,' Doris shouted.

Dressed in vanilla-white

My best girl friend's father made a pass at me. I'm eighteen and he's old – Gus is forty-three. I can't believe it happened. Particularly as I've known Gus ever since I was eleven and I've especially looked up to him. He has a soft voice and is the only older man who takes me seriously and really talks to me about life. He is rich and also a Communist. He explains about how and what Communism is and obviously feels very guilty about all his money. The means of production of his business shouldn't be owned by him, I guess, but for the moment they are. He is generous with his money, giving it to an important cause like medical aid to Mao Zedong's People's Liberation Army. I really love Gus like a father, that's why I agreed to meet him.

To make it clear – my folks have disowned me. I want to be a writer and not settle down with a doctor in Scarsdale, so I left home and refused to listen to my mom's constant warnings about my desire to explore 'life'. Now I share a room in Brooklyn with my second best girlfriend. However, I don't want to go into all that, but to tell you I am studying American Literature this summer at New York University and also work part-time at their bookstore near Greenwich Village. That was where I was when I received a telephone call from Gus, on a July afternoon. Harriet, his wife, and Dorothy, his daughter and my best friend, were down at the beach in Fire

Island and because of business he couldn't go out there until tomorrow. 'It's nice weather, so how about a ride on the Staten Island Ferry?' he said, and as he was Dorothy's father, I couldn't say No. Instead, I agreed to meet him at seven at the South Street Subway Station.

Gus was right. It was not the usual sweaty New York summer night, but airy with little currents of cool breezes touching you. Everyone was out on the street, a party evening. Girls dressed in ice-cream colors – strawberry-pink, mint-green, peach-yellow, mouth-watering shades. I wore vanilla-white.

It's only a ten-minute subway ride from Astor Place to South Street. Too bad Dorothy isn't here too, I thought, as I tried to calm myself down and not hear my mom's voice warning me about 'life'. My train pulled into the station and I could see through the dirty window that Gus was already waiting on the other side of the turnstile. I wobbled on my heels on to the platform and pushed through the exit to meet him.

'Judy, I'm so glad you could come,' and Gus took my hand, led me up the steps.

Outside, I took in a deep breath and with it childhood memories of summers by the ocean returned – the sharp smell of sea salt, the wild waves.

'Come on, Gus, I want to see the Hudson,' and I pulled him with me as if he were Dorothy. Together we ran across the street to the water's edge where the covered warehouses stood, the jetties reaching out into the river. It was quiet there except for the lapping water, the sometime hooting of the

Staten Island Ferry. We stood watching the tugs come inland for the night – how I longed for the open water, to fly with the seagulls to the ocean.

'Let's imagine we're going to Europe,' Gus suggested. He knew this was my dream and just mentioning it caused a film to run in my head with images of Paris – the Seine, the Eiffel Tower, the Louvre Palace. But what was Gus doing including himself in my future? I looked anxiously at him to see what he meant but he was just smiling, the cleft in his chin very noticeable. We strolled to the change-booth near the ferry and he took four dimes out of his pocket to pay for two round-trip tickets. I followed him up the gangplank. Whorls of dark water were being pushed out from under the ferry as we slowly moved out of the harbour towards the distant shore of Staten Island.

I was leaning against the iron railing finishing the last of my ham sandwich and coffee when suddenly my heart seized up. The wake of the ship was flecking out behind us and I understood that land was moving further away. I looked into Gus's white face, there were shadows where the lines ran from his nose to his mouth. His eyes were dark looking at me. I cleared my throat and began to talk. I talked incessantly, piling word upon word, building a wall of words to protect me from I didn't know what. I pointed out the many distant buildings of lower Manhattan, some in shadows and some brightly lit by electric stars. Then I realized they were like a phalanx of warriors guarding the approach home against me. I trembled in my vanilla-white dress.

'Would you like my jacket?' Gus asked gently and he took it off. I watched myself putting it on. All the obvious things were happening to me – racing heart, weak knees, and I couldn't control them. It was warm inside the jacket and I was helpless. He pushed back my flying hair and kissed me lightly on my lips. You're Dorothy's father, you're not supposed to do that, I shouted in my head.

'Sweet Judy,' and he kissed me again. His mouth soft against mine, kissing my hair, my cheeks, my mouth.

I wasn't supposed to be allowing this, so I had to shut up. I had a terrible war with my conscience – heard my mom's voice shouting about leaving home, getting into trouble. I couldn't enjoy the setting sun, the deepening summer sky, the movement of the boat running through the water. Not only did Gus kiss me, but also he talked about things dear to me and that made me happy and worried at the same time. Standing close to me, his soft voice whispered hope for my future, urging on my dreams of writing well, of one day becoming a published author. At times I thought the trip would never end, then suddenly the ferry was docking at South Street and it was over.

The air on shore was stifling. There was no further need for Gus's jacket. I returned it, thanking him politely for its use. He would take me home, so we plunged again down the stairs into the sweltering Subway. I had nothing to say. I felt limp with embarrassment and couldn't look at him. We stood silently waiting for the train.

There were other New Yorkers in the car with us returning

from their night out. For a long five minutes Gus and I sat next to each other on the stiff rattan seat, not speaking.

'Judy?'

I managed to look at him.

'Judy, don't be upset,' he spoke soothingly. I couldn't smile, so many things were happening inside me. He took my hands in his. 'You mustn't be upset. It was a lovely evening.' He spoke carefully, 'But it's not important. Things just happen,' he said. 'You'll understand when you're older.'

I watched his mouth moving, piling word upon empty word.

The Case is Altered

Mr. Justice Green closed the door and took off his judge's wig; he would be free until called. In the late June heat his head was itching, he had to scratch it. Of course he'd been thorough so the decision on the case wouldn't take long, and fortunately it was the last one for the week. After quickly drinking a glass of water, he took out his folded handkerchief to pat his mouth, then to further cool himself he flapped open and closed his long gown. The call came, the jury had returned. He scratched his damp hair again before putting on the wig.

Mr. Justice Green waited while the Foreman announced the unanimous verdict of the jury. They had found for the plaintiff. He was prepared for this decision, named the damage due and the session was declared closed. The courtroom began to empty, the doors were closed, his gown was handed over, and he carefully placed his wig in its own black box. David Green was now free, 'school'out until a week on Monday. While combing his damp hair, he looked at his thin face in the glass. Yes, he was tired but on top of things. Head of the class again. Across his mind flashed a woman's face – she was smiling at him.

On the gravel path outside the court, David nodded to a colleague, saw another waving to him. After three months as Circuit Court Judge, he was beginning to be recognised as one of them. And Judge Cook was walking towards him.

'David,' he called resonantly. 'How about a drink?'

David waited until the red face was near. 'I can't, Michael. Sorry. Mary's expecting me. We're off to France tomorrow.'

'How nice. Well, another time. Heard Savigny-les-Beaunes is good this year,' and he smiled. 'Have a good trip,' and he veered off across the street to 'The Case Is Altered'.

David walked towards his car. To drink in a crowded pub, discussing cricket or Cowes Week, didn't interest him. What a pleasure it would be to argue points of law over a glass of wine, but unfortunately that wasn't their thing. They were competent judges, good men and women, and he was now one of them.

He backed the Volvo out of its numbered parking space and on to the road. It was easy driving at the far edge of London, before he joined the North Circular. Moving slowly along the tree-lined secondary roads gave him time to think over the past three months and, summing up, he concluded that being a new judge had been testing. Happily, this first period was over and by tomorrow he and Mary would be away on the promise of eight days of touring through Picardy, the Aisne, where he would show his wife the cathedral.

Over twenty years had passed since he'd first visited Laon, seen the sculptured oxen on the cathedral. Heads tilted, nostrils flaring, the stone oxen peered down from their high medieval towers to watch the inevitable passing of men and women. In this way the stonemasons had paid homage to the living animals that pulled the carts up the volcanic hill to build the great church. The fundamental humanity had touched him then, so he'd felt eager to return. As he thought about it now, the visit could be labelled as sentimental nonsense. Did he really want to go back? Perhaps he wasn't thinking clearly because he was tired, and he decided to pull over and stop a moment. It was probably his confining pinstriped jacket that was bothering him, and he took it off. Yet, it was more than tiredness he felt, rather a feeling of high energy cut off.

David Green. Barrister. He had been so proud of that title. He closed his eyes and there he was back in his old chambers at the Inns of Court. The head clerk was at his usual seat and nearby his law colleagues were standing together to judge him. He heard them again speak their verdict: David Green was brilliant, except that all of his cases were settled out of court. He brought in no important money; thus there was no future for him in the chambers. He, the prize-winner, the Biblical Just Man, was to be abandoned, despaired of, judged wanting. So, the head clerk watched him, noted that he must leave. But this couldn't be the end of his career, David argued. He must rise. And with Mary, her friends, he began the long walk up the political pathways towards change. He left his chambers and at forty-eight was chosen by his political party to don the black silk breeches, the white stockings, the new horsehair wig of the judge.

David opened his eyes. Why had he gone over that nightmare again? The past was over; there was only his new and successful life to enjoy. Right now at home in Highgate, Mary was busy making certain that the right clothes for their holiday were packed. During their seven years of marriage, he could always count on her doing the right thing. Yes, life was as it should be now and he again started the engine.

Driving on, he saw he'd taken a different road home. Rather than continue around the North Circular to Highgate from Whipps Cross, he was beginning to go down Blackhorse Road. Four o'clock. Yes, of course he had mentioned to Mary that on his way home he might go via Stoke Newington, drop in to say hello to old friends. He hadn't seen Eleanor for ages, she'd probably be working at home. Would Tom still be teaching at college? Well, he'd have a short visit with them, just a cup of tea and a quick chat about the time when they were young and together visited the Cathedral at Laon.

Weaving his way through Tottenham was an adventure he could do without, but it was the price he'd have to pay for going this way. Music might offset the bleakness, the endless Allsop, Bennet, Gershon 'For Sale' signs that hung over the closed shops. He fumbled, then pushed in a random CD. With the first three bars the air in the car was ignited with the love song between Siegfried and Brunhilde. He knew it well. *Zu neuen Taten, teurer Helde,* she sang.

People kept crossing the streets, disregarding the rushing cars, the lights. Shabby people shouting, bargaining over the price of tomatoes, broccoli, yams. This wild contradiction pitted against the glory of Wagner's music distracted him. He must concentrate. How he treasured the two voices possessed by passion, by power, so much better to erase the compromised present, become intoxicated by the rapturous sounds. No. No, he mustn't think this. Yet the ecstatic crescendo of the music defied his reason and he joined the soaring voices in the climax. Then stillness followed. In his mind, a woman's face rose. Just in time he saw the red light.

'Wash?' A black face peered in at the window, wielding a squeegee.

'What?' David fumbled to turn off the CD. He watched the circling soapy water and told the man to stop. With the windscreen half-wiped, David stepped on the pedal to continue on until he finally turned down Church Street.

The music had moved him too much. The appointment to meet Eleanor and Tom was a one-off. It was good that Mary knew about Eleanor, that allowed him and Tom to continue their friendship from Manchester Grammar School days. Tom's past political rhetoric and his own cool reason had been at odds at times, but they always enjoyed their disagreements. He slowed the car down as it approached the blue door, number twenty-two, and stopped.

David felt an extra heartbeat. Not because of being here, he insisted and stepped outside, closing the car door. Passing down the small garden, he pressed the bell, heard it ringing through the house as he stood by the white rose bush. Silence. He heard no footsteps. Eleanor wasn't there. She was too busy, or had forgotten. Well that was too bad, like a gift lost. David turned towards his car, felt a cavernous space inside him. He took out his handkerchief, wiped his face.

He acknowledged she was needed. Her brown hair with the streaks of grey would partially hide her face as she poured the tea, cut the raisined Boodle cake. She would lightly mention her stories written for children, her worried concern for them in today's everything-available world. He would listen, say nothing, as he and Mary had no children. Perhaps he'd come with Mary another time, David reminded himself as he opened the car door.

Inside, he folded his arms on the wheel. He'd go in a minute. Eleanor. He knew the unanswered ache of Wagner's song was read in his face, his body, but he would not translate it into a word. The saying of it was not possible. He started up the engine. Backing up, David saw in the rear mirror that Eleanor was walking down the hill towards him. She was wearing a cornflower blue dress. Oh, God, God. He was trembling – his heart adding extra beats.

The Geography Lesson

Joan put down the bright blue crayon after marking in the Mississippi on her Geography map. It was fun drawing the movement of the long river as it snaked from the freezing State of Minnesota down to the warm Gulf of Mexico. There across the aisle, Tommy was making yellow strokes, filling Kansas with wheat, and at the far side of the class Mark would be busy finishing his map because he was always first. She imagined his glasses misting over with laughter as he raised his hand high above his head, then dropping his red crayon to dot Washington State with a rash of apples. Since they first started school, Joan appreciated his daring.

She took up her crayon, wrote in orange letters at the top of the paper: Joan Taylor, Age 10, Class 6A. Geography Map of the United States of America, May 6th, 1939. After finishing, she wondered if she should put in the grey circles for Alabama cotton and turned to look for Mr Simon, her favourite teacher. He'd been called out of class but now was returning with a boy about her age, who was wearing, of all things, grey leather shorts. Joan saw the other children had also stopped working to look, and she caught her friend Barbara's smile.

Mr Simon stood in front of the big globe on his desk with the boy by his side, waiting for attention. 'Children, I want you to meet a new pupil. This is Ulrich Held … Oolee for short. He will be coming to this school. He has come alone all the way from Germany, which you know is very far away, and he doesn't speak English.'

Joan listened as Mr Simon pointed to the big map on the wall with its pink, blue, green, brown countries. He explained about brown Germany, its iron and coal, the steel for heavy industry used for trains, cars and big guns. Then she lost interest and listened to the running and shouting voices outside, as the older children from 7B played 'capture the flag'. In a few minutes she'd be outside for a short recess, and wondered which game she'd be playing.

Oolee was jiggling about trying to stuff his fat hands into the narrow pockets of his shorts, but they wouldn't fit and Joan covered her mouth to hide a laugh. For a second he looked straight at her, then his eyes moved on to watch Tommy, Mark and Barbara, never stopping for long but peering hard, until he had gone into all the children's faces. Finished, he rubbed his nose, then wiped the wet on his pants. The colour darkened the leather and Joan knew Oolee hadn't a hanky. Now he was looking down and she saw his white eyebrows pop up – it was clear one of the two buttons that closed the front flap to his shorts had broken off, was gone. A funny look came on Oolee's face as she watched his fingers creep across his tummy, pull at the last button to see if it held.

Joan had never seen anyone like him before. Why was his dirty blonde hair cut so very short, making his ears stand out like big mushrooms? He had little blue eyes, a fat body and his feet were in yellow square-toed shoes. The class was also watching and she looked up at Mr Simon to see what he would say after he finished his Geography talk.

'Children, Oolee is new here but he wants to be your friend. Now, please say hello to Oolee.'

They all got up, shuffling together to make a half-circle. Joan looked across to Barbara, and with one voice they all called out, 'Hello Oolee'. Again Joan smiled at Barbara and together they again called, 'Hello Oolee,' pulling out the vowels like chewing gum. One by one the other children joined them, 'Hehlooo Ooooleeee, Hehloooo Ooooleeee.' The name grew louder and louder until it circled Mr Simon's globe, reaching up to the maps on the walls.

Joan's voice went higher, chanting, and there was Oolee tucking his chin inside his shirt like a tortoise, his arms flapping. Mr Simon was standing stiff as a stick, his brown eyes wide open and on his face a funny expression. Then he pulled Oolee to him, closed his arms around him. Still her voice shrieked with the others, 'Oolee, Oolee, Oolee.'

A stinky smell came and she looked around for the one who did it. Tears were running down Oolee's face and they all knew he had done a number two in his leather shorts. Suddenly Mr Simon took off his jacket, wrapped it around Oolee's body and half lifted him out of the classroom.

She continued calling his name, but after a while she became tired, couldn't be bothered any more. One by one, the others also stopped. It was boring to stand in a half-circle and Joan went to sit down at her desk. Barbara put her head on her arms. Mark wiped his glasses, while Tommy and the others kept standing.

Outside, the end of 7B's recess came with shouts of, 'All, All in Free', but no one came to dismiss 6A, send them outside. Should she ask a teacher what to do, Joan wondered? The clock moved, still no one came. Mr Simon usually read to them before they went home, a wonderful voyage about *Jason and the Golden Fleece*. Would he read to them again?

Footsteps, Mr Simon opened the door and came in. Without looking at anyone, he told the children to put their work away, put chairs on the desks. He sat at his desk, gathered his books together and placed them one by one in his briefcase.

Joan lifted the desk lid, put away her crayons and map of the United States. Her arms felt weak and the chair heavy when she lifted it.

'Class dismissed,' Mr Simon said to the wall. The others finished and quickly left.

Joan reached down to pick up her satchel and there on the floor was Oolee's button. It was rough against her finger, and she looked around not knowing what to do. She got up, slowly went over to Mr Simon's desk and put it down.

'His button,' she said, 'it's broken.'

Thank you to the monthly writers'group meeting at Festival Hall for their tactful and useful help, to the many teachers at The City Lit, Emma Cuthbert for her book cover design, Victor Castano for his technical help, Dr. Winifred Stevenson for her editorial assistance and patient Robert Dourmashkin for his continuous support.

SYDNEE BLAKE was born in New York, lived in France but has spent most of her working life in London. She has been an actor, theatre director and teacher. Her stories have appeared in *Worldwide Writers*, *Brittle Star* and have placed in awards including The Ian St James, The New Writer and Fish. She has two sons and four grandchildren.